McPHEE GRIBBLE/PENGUIN BOOKS

MILK

Beverley Farmer was born in Melbourne in 1941 and educated at MacRobertson Girls' High School and Melbourne University. She has supported herself since through a variety of jobs, mainly teaching, dishwashing and waitressing. For three years in Greece she lived a village life, taught English and helped run a seaside restaurant. Her stories have been widely published and have won many awards. *Alone*, her first novel was published in 1980. Beverley Farmer lives in Lorne on the south-west coast of Victoria with her eleven year-old son. At present she is writing full-time.

MILK

stories by
BEVERLEY FARMER

Published with the assistance of the
Literature Board of the Australia Council

McPHEE GRIBBLE / PENGUIN BOOKS

McPhee Gribble Publishers Pty Ltd
66 Cecil Street
Fitzroy, Victoria, 3065, Australia

Penguin Books Australia Ltd,
487 Maroondah Highway, P.O. Box 257
Ringwood, Victoria, 3134, Australia
Penguin Books Ltd,
Harmondsworth, Middlesex, England
Penguin Books,
40 West 23rd Street, New York, N.Y. 10010, U.S.A.
Penguin Books Canada Ltd,
2801 John Street, Markham, Ontario, Canada
Penguin Books (N.Z.) Ltd,
182-190 Wairau Road, Auckland 10, New Zealand

First published by McPhee Gribble Publishers
in association with Penguin Books Australia, 1983
Reprinted 1984, twice
Copyright © Beverley Farmer, 1983

Typeset in Bembo by Bookset, Melbourne
Made and printed in Australia by
The Dominion Press—Hedges & Bell

National Library of Australia
Cataloguing-in-Publication data

Farmer, Beverley, 1941–
Milk, stories.
ISBN 014 007184 9
I. Title.
A823.3

Γιά τό Χρῆστο, γιά πολλούς λόγους.

«῍Ολοι γιά προσώρας εἴμαστε ὅπου καί να πᾶμε...»

'All of us are passing through no matter where we go ...'
Stratis Myrivilis, *The Mermaid Madonna*

ACKNOWLEDGEMENTS

Acknowledgement is made to the publications in which these stories first appeared:

'Milk' in *Island*, 1983; 'Melpo' in the *Bulletin*, 1982; 'Sally's Birthday' in the *Sun-Herald*, 1982 (winner of the 1981 *Sun-Herald* Short Story Competition); 'Ismini' in *Westerly*, 1982; 'Darling Odile' in *Cleo*, 1982; 'Gerontissa' in *Tabloid Story* (*Nation Review*), 1980; 'Snake' in *Meanjin*, 1982; 'Pumpkin' in *Jetaway*, 1983; 'Inheritance' in *Westerly*, 1982; 'The Captain's House' in the *Age*, 1983 (one of six winners in the *Age/Tabloid Story* Award, 1982); 'Maria's Girl' in *Tabloid Story* (*National Times*), 1982

The author appreciates the assistance of a grant from The Literature Board of the Australia Council.

CONTENTS

MILK

I was nine when my father first took me to Greece for a summer. He came from a northern village. There were, as he had promised, animals everywhere. And my grandparents did love me. Yiayia, my grandmother, read me stories and spoiled me. My grandfather, Pappou, was deaf, so we didn't talk much. But he took me everywhere. My cousins, the other grandchildren, all lived in the city and were only visiting. Sometimes they were nice, sometimes they teased me. They picked fights. They sulked.

'Niko's our boy,' Yiayia said. 'He's flown thousands of miles just to be with us. So don't be mean.' They groaned. 'You all have mothers,' she added. 'Niko hasn't. His died when he was three.'

When they'd gone home it was better. As well as feeding the animals we did heavy work in the fields, Pappou and I. I helped load bales of lucerne and hay on the cart, and lay the pipes for watering, and hoe the tobacco. My father helped too. I wanted us to stay for ever, but he said no.

*

My father and I took Pappou to the market town and bought him a cow with a calf. Whatever we and the calf couldn't drink, Yiayia could make into cheese or yoghurt, or sell. Not many people in the village had a cow then, though there were goats and sheep with pink bags of milk between their legs. Our cow, all hide and bones, had an udder so huge that she looked, Yiayia said, as if she was perched on a barrel. She was put in the barn next to the house with her calf and Pappou's old horse. I helped with the milking. We let the calf suck first, to start the milk flowing. When we hauled him away, the calf propped and pranced and the cow gazed round in dismay, both of them mooing. After the milking we set the calf free to finish off. Once in his rush he knocked Pappou over in a pile of wet black dung. I shrieked with joy. Pappou sat there and cursed me.

'Niko! Niko!' Yiayia was furious. I blushed and said sorry to Pappou. He was looking sheepishly at me. Niko was his name too, of course. I was named after him. Who did she mean? Bemused, we looked at her. She laughed then.

*

Yiayia asked me to hang up the curd cheeses at night in their white cloths, high up on a pole near the grapevine that shaded the porch, so that cats and dogs couldn't snatch them. I wished I didn't have to. Up there near the porch lamp beetles rattled against me as I tied knots. Cobwebs clung. The whey dripped in my eyes and down my arms.

'Good boy,' Yiayia said. 'That's fine. Up there nothing will get them. Not even the wolf.'

The wolf. My cousins had told me horror stories about a wolf: a *lykanthropos*, a werewolf that they said lived in the village.

'Is there one here, Yiayia?'

'Lots. Ooooh.' She made a howl and laughed up at me, her eyes lost in yellow wrinkles. 'Not in summer, silly. There are in winter.'

'Why?'

'Why? It snows here, that's why. They get hungry.'

'Where are they now?'

'Up on the mountain. And there they'll stay till you've gone home, so you can get down now.'

I slipped down. The mountain hunched grey beyond the river, the lights of its villages twinkling and fading like fireflies.

'Have you ever seen one, Yiayia?'

'One or two. There was one last winter as big as the calf. It was full moon like now, but on snow, so I saw it clearly through the window. The men went after it with guns. You'd have shot it for us, eh, cowboy?' She said it in English, *kaouboyee*. 'It'll be back.'

'Did it kill anything?'

'It couldn't get in. The foxes were worse. It only came for the donkeys.'

'How did it get in?'

'Oh, not in a barn, no. On the other side of the river. They were tied.'

'In the snow?'

'Yes, poor things.'

'*Why?*'

'What use is a donkey in winter? There's no room, no feed. They say it's cheaper to buy a new one in spring.'

'So they feed the old ones to the wolf?'

Yiayia shook her head. That meant yes. No was when she tossed her head back, frowned and said tsk.

'They didn't have to tie them,' I whispered.

'Yes, they did, or they'd have come home.'

I gazed in horror.

'If you aren't your father all over again!' she said. 'Here in winter there's nothing all round but snow and ice. People die too.'

'I'd go and untie them!'

'God love you,' she said. 'They'd die anyway.'

'I'd feed them!'

But she'd gone in. Layers of mist were floating blue and silver over the rooftops. I shivered. The porch lamp blinked. Cobwebs full of beetles hung from it. The muddy cups of swallows' nests were empty of birds. Dogs barked. It seemed to me that the night had a chill already.

A fat donkey jiggled past. The rider, her face turned away from our house, was Kyria Tassoula.

*

Kyria Tassoula never spoke to my grandmother. It was some old quarrel, my father said. Women and their quarrels. Her house was just over the road. Some of the family would say hullo as I went past, but as if it embarrassed them to, so I mumbled and scuffled on. Their boy Stelio liked me.

One afternoon, too hot to sleep – we all slept after lunch – I found an old woman in the kitchen with Yiayia eating yoghurt. She hobbled over to me, peering hard, and patted my cheek. Her breath was sour. Like all the old women, except Yiayia, she was wrinkled, toothless, all wrapped in black. They were talking, but it wasn't Greek. I ate some yoghurt and watched them. Yiayia dressed in colours and left her white hair uncovered in a bun bright as a snowball in sunlight. Only close up her red cheeks were cracked with lines. She smelled of rosewater.

She told me later that that was Stelio's grandmother, his father's mother. She sometimes came over in secret and if she wasn't well enough they kept in touch through a neighbour. She was Kyria Tassoula's mother-in-law, but she hated her too. She was glad I was friends with Stelio.

I wasn't really. Stelio, though bigger and older – nearly fourteen – had played soccer by the river some evenings with me and my cousins. Once, seeing that I was fascinated by the fireflies, he chased and caught me one. In the red ridges of his palm it glowed weakly, a little battered grub.

'What is it in English?' he grinned. He was a greasy boy, always grinning, heavy yet loose and light-footed.

'Firefly.'

'Fyah flyee. Fyah flyee.'

He walked home with us, so I had to keep the firefly. From the corner he lagged behind. Frightened of his stepmother, my cousins whispered. Kyria Tassoula, she beats him, and she beats his father too, and one day you'll have a stepmother, too, Niko. I hoped not.

*

There were always night noises. Cats fought on roof-tops, roosters crowed at the moon, donkeys burst out in sudden sobs and groans. Tractors roared past from day-break, then the early bus. When, that night, frantic yells and snorts woke me I thought, I hoped, it was just a donkey. I thought of the *lykanthropos*. My father ran to open the shutters. The screaming blasted in then, loud, agonized.

'What is it, Dad?'

'I don't know.'

Yiayia and Pappou were on the porch staring over at the yard of Stelio's house, where torches glowed and thrust agile shadows among men and thistles.

'It's all right,' Pappou said. 'It's only a donkey. Tassoula's donkey. *Yennaei*.'

Laying an egg. I knew that word. But Stelio's step-mother's donkey wasn't. It was shrieking with pain.

'Oh my God!' my father said. 'Can't they do something?'

'Tsk. Not now. It's finished. Listen to it.'

Lights went on in house after house. Dogs barked.

'If they bring a *haïvan-doktor*?'

'Tsk. Too late.'

I clutched my father's arm.

'Oh God. Why don't they shoot it?'

'Them?' Yiayia grinned. 'You don't think they'd waste a bullet? Slit its throat maybe. That's more like it.'

'Sssh, Sevasti,' Pappou said.

'It's my bet she poisoned it.'

'Sssh.' Pappou took her inside and turned out the lights. My father locked our shutters. In the dark I crawl-ed into bed with him and he made room, one arm tightly round me. The screams and sobs were quieter after a while.

'She's getting better, Dad,' I said. 'Isn't she?'

'Yes,' he said. 'Go to sleep.'

'What was wrong with her?'

'It's over now. Sleep.'

The bed smelled of my father, as he smelled when we were in Greece. Of sweat and dust and hay.

*

In the morning, helping Yiayia to search the barn for eggs, I found out the truth. The donkey had not got better. It was gone. At first light it was carted to the hill.

'*Pethane, totes?*' It died, then? I still wasn't sure.

'*Psofise*, little one,' she said. 'Not *pethane.*'

'*Psofise?*'

'*Pethane* is for when people die.'

'What if you say *psofise* when people die?'

'No, you mustn't, it's an insult.'

'Then it's an insult for animals too.'

'Don't be silly,' she said. 'People are more than animals. People have souls.'

'Well I'm saying *pethane.*'

'Tsk.'

I had to see for myself. I sauntered past their yard and just glanced in. The tall thistles were all trampled and torn up. There in the midst of them stood the grey donkey. *Den pethane*, I said aloud, it didn't die, so there. It trotted to me, breathing hoarsely, and pushed its gazing head through the barbed wire. It came up to my middle. At last I understood. It was a baby, a newborn *gaïdouraki*. I rushed home and told her.

'I think it's hungry,' I added.

It was sure to be. It had stayed by the mother's corpse all night and sucked it. My skin prickled.

'Will the wolf eat the mother, Yiayia?'

The wolf or something else. Weren't they all God's creatures?

'Yiayia, can I please feed the *gaïdouraki*? There's plenty of milk!'

It was too small. It was best to forget it.

'With a baby bottle, please, Yiayia, I know how!'

No, it was a waste of time. It wasn't ours. Stelio's stepmother would stop me. The whole village would laugh at us both. But she gave in and wearily found me an old bottle with a teat and handed it to me to fill with warm milk.

The *gaïdouraki* stumbled to me with little sobs and wheezes. I held his head. At first his lips fumbled, then they clamped on the teat. As he gulped I stroked his fluffy back with the dark cross on it. His eyes watched, river-brown eyes lined with black. I patted his rough nose.

'What are you up to, Niko?'

Stelio was always there before you saw him.

'It's hungry, isn't it? What's its name?'

'Hasn't got one, silly.'

'What'll we call it?' I asked him. It was their donkey.

'I know!' He grinned. 'Fyah Flyee.'

'Firefly. All right.' I liked it. Stelio laughed. When the bottle was empty I climbed out. Through the wires Firefly nudged me, panting. I looked back. Stelio waved.

*

On the next market day Pappou and my father went on the bus but I stayed home to feed Firefly. Preparing his bottles – he was becoming insatiable – I chattered on to Yiayia, though as usual she wasn't listening. She often wasn't happy. She had been very quiet all that day. As I turned to go she put her hand on my shoulder.

'Wait. Are you going over there?'

I just looked at her.

'Well, look, do something for me, eh? Will you, Niko? Stelio's grandmother's sick in bed. Take her this yoghurt.'

'Yiayia, I *can't*. I've never been to the house. I go to the yard not the –'

'Stelio's your friend,' she said. 'His stepmother went on the bus, I saw her. I can't go, you know that. Come on, Niko, you do it for a donkey, won't you do it for a poor sick old woman? Niko, please?'

I left the bowl with its embroidered cloth over it on a fence post while I fed Firefly, and Stelio found it.

'What's this, Niko?'

'Oh. It's for your grandmother.'

'What's in it?'

'Yoghurt.'

'What?' He had a look. 'Yoghurt for my grandmother?'

'She's sick, isn't she?'

'She's sick, so what? We've got food.'

'Oh.' What would Yiayia say?

'You idiot, take it home. What next? Ha ha.' His voice when he laughed was a yodel. 'See if Firefly wants it.' Firefly poked his head between my legs and Stelio doubled up. 'See! He thinks that you're his mother. Ha ha ha! You are now, aren't you, Niko?'

*

I hoped Yiayia would give up then, but no. She would take the yoghurt herself, but I had to come and carry it. She ignored my whining protests. Stelio gaped when he saw who had knocked, but he led us in politely and left us there. It was hot in the dark inner room, its windows and shutters all locked. There was a bad smell. Yiayia kissed the head lying above a tangle of dim sheets. 'Sophia,' she murmured. I heard an answering croak, but I understood nothing of what they said. When Yiayia said '*Yiaourti*,' I stepped forward with it.

'*Ligo*,' the voice struggled. A little. '*Ligo*, Sevasti.'

Yiayia went to look for a spoon. I hurried after her. She stopped short. Kyria Tassoula stood there, Stelio behind her.

'You?' she said to Yiayia. 'You sneak in here when I'm out, do you?' Then she saw the bowl. 'And what's that?'

'Yoghurt,' I whispered. 'For Stelio's grandmother.'

'*What?*' Kyria Tassoula grabbed it, strode into the bedroom with it and hurled all the yoghurt on the bare floor. It splashed in lumps like vomit.

'You old fool!' she said. 'You beg food from *her*, do you? Then eat it.' She swung round to us. 'You think no one else can make yoghurt?'

'*Fonissa*,' hissed Yiayia. I didn't know that word.

'Get out. You and your brat.' She gave me the bowl. 'Mad old women.' She smiled. 'Do you find each other by the smell?' Stelio's laughter whooped.

Yiayia said nothing on the way home. She locked all the doors and shut herself in her bedroom. No one was home. I sat in the silence praying that my father would come soon. In the end I made coffee, thick and sweet, I knew how, and took it in to her. She drank it. She was crying. My father and Pappou, when at last the bus came back, sent me to hang up the cheeses while she told them. When I'd finished, Yiayia was whimpering into my father's shoulder. Pappou sat grey and stiff.

'Tassoula came home in the bread van,' he was saying.

'When I was little,' Yiayia said, as if she hadn't heard, 'I thought she was a princess. Sophia's clothes! Her braided hair! In church the priest couldn't think straight.' Her yellow lips shook. 'You should see her now. I've kissed corpses with more life in them.'

Kissed corpses. My own grandmother.

'She says Tassoula's poisoning her,' Yiayia said, 'and she won't eat or drink. *Fonissa einai*, she said.'

'Since when?' asked my father.

'Since the night the donkey died.'

'What!'

'She said it was a sign.'

'Mama, you know that's nonsense,' my father said. 'She's sick, she's dying of cancer, haven't they told her?'

Cancer was a word I knew. *Karkino*. My mother had died of that. It was something inside you that ate you, not like a worm, like a giant wart. You couldn't catch it from anyone who had it. You died slowly.

'Is hungry sick, *paidi mou*?' Yiayia's lips stretched in a yellow grin. 'Is hunger a cancer? Is it? That's what she's dying of.'

'Mama, she has cancer. The doctor told me.'

'Tassoula wants her dead, that's all I know.' She looked at Pappou, who looked down.

'Mama, if she won't eat —'

'She would have eaten the yoghurt.'

*

The house over the road had a horror in it now. Not during the day, just as the cemetery had none then, but lay there sunny and green beside the gravel road that led to our tobacco fields, its stone crosses crowded by thistles with mauve flowers and the singing of furred brown bees. After dark came the horror. Rattling home in the cart I could never look at the cemetery, and to shut my eyes was worse. I gazed ahead at Marko, Pappou's horse. I saw nothing but Marko's bouncing rump and the swung black hair of his mane and tail. We turned at the church, its storks' nest sprawled on the tower. Then past Stelio's house with a clatter. I looked away. At last, our own bright porch.

That night I was in the fetid room again. An indistinct shape in the bed mewed words I didn't know. Yiayia sobbed. Kyria Tassoula leapt into the darkness. Pale yoghurt splashed. I begged for the light to stay on. My father said no, it would bring every mosquito in the village. So he let me come into bed with him and talk till I felt better.

I asked him what *fonissa* meant. I thought it might be something like *lykanthropos*. Kyria Tassoula had pointed eyeteeth and, in my dream, gold eyes.

'A *fonissa*,' he said, 'is a woman who kills someone. A murderess.' He hesitated. 'Your Yiayia was very angry when she said that, Nick. She didn't mean it, you know.' I didn't answer. 'You mustn't talk to people about it. All right?'

'Yes.' He turned over. 'Dad? Did my mother – smell like that?'

'*What?*'

'That old lady smells – dirty.'

'Oh no. God, no. Your mother was in hospital. The nurses took good care of her. Jesus Christ.'

'Why doesn't Stelio's grandmother go to hospital?'

'Well, only people who might get better go to hospital here. If they're too sick they come home. She's lived in that house for fifty years. She'd be frightened anywhere else.'

'She's frightened of Kyria Tassoula.'

'No, no. She doesn't like her, that's all.' I said nothing. 'She gave you a fright, I know. She has a bad temper. But that doesn't make her a *fonissa*.'

'Yiayia said –'

'I know. But Tassoula does her best. Most people do, Nick. That's what I think.'

'Yiayia doesn't think she has cancer, does she?'

'You can't change an old mind. It's no use trying. So go to sleep, Nick, will you? It's three o'clock.'

*

Yiayia gave up. The next couple of days she woke late, and in the afternoon heat when we went to bed she lay crying. My father prepared meals. The dirty washing rose out of its basket like dough. Yiayia wouldn't help with the milking, but sat inside while Pappou clashed buckets and cursed. She groaned, the second day, when he brought the milk in, that milk was more a burden than a blessing. Pappou hurled it, bucket and all, through the kitchen window. We had none to drink. I gave Firefly water. When we came in from the fields that evening we found her in the last red light from the window, peeling potato after potato into a pan of water. Again, nothing was cooking. On the table at her elbow a hen flounced and jabbed at crumbs. Yiayia's cheeks were wet. Pappou and my father bent over her.

I found Firefly gasping with hunger, grieving.

'Yiayia!' I burst in, frantic. 'There must be some milk somewhere!'

'Are you thirsty, little one?' she droned.

'For the *gaïdouraki*, Yiayia.'

'Ach. You and your *gaïdouraki*.'

'Please, Yiayia.'

'Come on, Nick, don't bother Yiayia,' my father said in English.

'The *gaïdouraki*,' Yiayia muttered. 'Why should I feed their *gaïdouraki*?'

'It's starving,' I said in English, and burst into sobs. 'And it's bloody not fair!'

'Nick, that's enough!'

Pappou, plodding in for a bucket, looked at me.

'What's wrong with our boy, eh?' he said.

'*Aman!* That *gaïdouraki*,' Yiayia snapped. '*People* can starve there and no one will lift a finger.'

'You want some milk, is that it?' I shook my head. 'Come and help and I'll give you some.' He patted my shoulder and bent over Yiayia, but I heard. '*Ela*, don't be hard on the boy, Sevasti *mou*. He's going soon.'

I stared at my father.

'Are we going soon?'

'Of course. You know we are.'

'When?'

'The day after tomorrow.'

'*No!*'

'Yes, we have to, Nick.'

In the barn I was not much use, but Pappou gave me the milk. I asked if he needed a donkey. No, he had a horse. He slapped its rump. He had no room, no feed, no use for a donkey. He said he was sorry. He was, I saw.

It was dark in the yard by then. Stelio was chasing Firefly with whoops and cracks of a whip. I said hullo. He stopped short with a giggle.

'Fyah Flyee. Here's mummy with your milky.'

He went on, though, cornering Firefly at last and trying to mount and ride him. When at last I had a chance to give him the bottles, he gobbled them and pressed hot and shaking against me.

'He loves his mummy,' Stelio sneered. 'Did you miss me yesterday, Niko?'

I shook my head and grinned back at his oily face.

'Know something, Niko?'

'What?'

'Your grandmother's mad. Everyone knows that.'

'Do they.'

'You know what else?'

'What?'

'If my father sees you here again he'll shoot you.'

That was a lie too. They didn't waste bullets. Besides

his stepmother beat them both. I wished I could watch.

'You're going home this week, I hear. Poor Fyah Flyee.' He pulled up one long soft ear and crouched to yell. 'You hear that? Your mummy's going home.'

'Will *you* look after him, Stelio?' I wheedled, but sick, hopeless. 'Look, he likes you.' Firefly cringed.

'Me? *I*'m not a donkey's mother.'

I picked up the bottles. He was still hungry. Would I dare come back with more? Stelio's chant followed me home.

'Niko's Fyah Flyee's mother. Niko's a donkey's mother. Eh, Niko?'

He saw me turn by the porch lamp.

'Niko, *tha psofisei, xereis?*'

Niko, he'll die, you know? I knew.

'I'll eat him alive! I'm a *lykanthropos.* Ooooh!' He laughed, howling. I went straight to bed.

*

The next day, our last, Stelio's grandmother died. Her corpse would stay at home until the funeral, my father said. If I met any of the family I was to shake hands and say sadly, '*Zoï se sas,*' long life to you. But I kept well away. Yiayia, her face like iron, sat on the porch watching a file of old people shuffle into Stelio's house. Finally she went herself. No one spoke to her or tried to stop her, she told Pappou. Who would have dared? I wondered if she kissed the corpse. She came back remote and eerie, a listless stranger, even her cheeks pale, and her white bun loose in wisps. She sighed, pouring me milk.

'It's my fault,' she murmured. 'I meant well. Am I to blame? But no one was a better friend to Sophia than I was.'

'They wouldn't let you help her.'

'Even so.'

'Yiayia.' I clutched the bottle and in spite of myself said it. '*To gaïdouraki mou tha pethanei.*'

'Ach, little one, yes.' She hugged me. 'Yes. *Tha psofisei*, poor thing. Ach, Niko *mou*.'

'*Yiati tha pethanei*, Yiayia? *Yiati?*' Why? But my last hope, gone.

'What can we do? It has to be so. We all have to die. We die, and donkeys die, even wolves die.' Tears shone in her eyes. 'Your own mother died, on the far side of the world, and I thought I'd go mad when they told me.' She smiled, a difficult smile. 'And you're a big strong brave boy now.'

For the last time I brought water in buckets to the cow, the calf and the horse. I hung the cheeses high among the cobwebs. I fed Firefly five times, the last time at night, a hard cold night with stars. I didn't see Stelio again. Candlelight moved behind their shutters. A dog howled. The mountain crouched black, spangled, a new moon above it.

We stayed up late after the bags were packed and we'd had dinner and drunk our milk and honey. My father and grandparents talked for so long, I woke in bed with my father at dawn before I knew I'd slept. We had coffee, all of us yellow and rumpled under the lightbulb, trying to hurry, but when we carried our bags to the bus stop the porch lamp was a blotch on the wall and the morning hot and white. Firefly's head was bowed through the wires. He moaned when he saw me coming. Even after we turned the corner I could hear. When the bus came Yiayia, in tears, kissed us goodbye. Pappou hugged her.

'They'll be back, they'll be back,' he said. 'Won't you, Niko?'

'No,' I said.

It made them smile.

MELPO

When I married Magda, Jimmy is thinking, all our family danced. We roasted kids and lambs in our whitewashed oven outside. We drank ouzo and new wine by the demijohn. The whole village was there. My mother had cooked everything. Cheese pies the size of cartwheels, meatballs, *pilafia* . . . In spring she picked nettles and dandelions and stewed them with rice, for Lent. In autumn she brewed thick jams from our apples and figs and windfall apricots. Tubs of yoghurt and curd cheese sat wrapped all day in blankets by our stove. On feast days an aged hen seethed, tawny and plump, in the pot. Until the Germans came, and then the Civil War.

The day I married Magda, my mother led the line of dancers holding the handkerchief, making her leaps and turns barefoot on the earth of our yard, by the light of kerosene lamps.

When our family planted out tobacco seedlings in the dry fields a long cart-ride from the village, we started at daybreak and rested in the heat of the afternoon under the oak trees at the spring. We ate hard bread, and cheese and olives, and drank spring water. Once when I was small I picked up a tortoise where it lumbered among pale clods of earth. It hissed, spurting hot urine on my hands. I dropped it, then picked it up again. *Mi*, Dimitraki! my old aunts shrieked in their black scarves. Melpo! *E*, Melpo! But my mother lay there with earthen feet, in shade as cold and thick as the spring water, fast asleep. My mother. Melpo . . .

'Now your mother wants to meet me,' Kerry is saying. 'Why now?'

Kerry looks taut, as if angry, Jimmy thinks; but she is only disconcerted. Flecked with brown, her pale face is blushing. A green glow off the water, wavering up, lights her bronze hair.

'Darling, she didn't say.'

'Well, why do you think she does?'

'She said so.'

'Yes, but why?'

'She didn't say.'

Jimmy, balancing his rod on the warm concrete of the pier, lies back, his head in Kerry's lap, his heavy eyes closed against the falling sun, the swathed still sea.

'You know she wouldn't hear of it before.'

'She asked me your name again and said, "Dimitri, you sure you want to marry this woman? Really marry, in our church?" '

'And what did you say?'

'Kerry.'

'Oh yes.'

'And yes, Mama, really marry.'

'What have you told her about me?'

'Nothing much. Red hair, I said. Australian, not Greek. Divorced, with one son called Ben. A teacher of maths at the same school where I teach Greek and –'

'Did you say anything about the baby?'

'No. Not yet.'

'Well, I'm not showing yet.'

'No.' He hesitates. 'Eleni and Voula have not told her either. I asked them.'

'They *know*?'

'Well, yes. I told *them*, they're my sisters. They said they'd guessed, anyway.'

'Oh, come on.'

'Yes. When they met you at the dance. They like to think they can always tell. They are pleased. A daddy at forty-five, they keep saying. Better late than never. They like you. How about after school on Thursday? Is that all right? Nothing formal. Just in and out.'

'All right.'

'You're blushing.'

'I'm nervous.'

'Try out your Greek on her.'

'I hope you're joking.'

'Me? I never joke.'

'You said she speaks English!'

'She does. She even makes us look words up for her. She hardly ever speaks Greek now, strangely enough. But very broken English. Nothing like mine. Mine is not bad, after only twenty years here. Would you not agree?'

'For a quiet life, why not?'

Shafts of sunlight are throbbing through the water as outspread fingers do, in fan-shapes.

'She wants to meet you now,' he sighs, 'because she is dying.'

'Oh! You've told her!'

'She wanted to know. I think she knew, anyway. Don't be shocked when you see her. She is wasting away, and her mind wanders. I wish you could have known her when she was young. Her life has been – *martyrio*. *Martyrio*, you know?'

'Martyrdom?'

'Yes. Martyrdom.'

'Because of the War?'

'Oh, yes, the War. Many things. The War was the worst. I was only about eight then. My sisters were too little to help. Our baby brother was sick. We were evacuated from our village. My father was a prisoner. Can you imagine it? His mother, my Yiayia Eleni, minded the little ones. I sold cigarettes, razor blades, *koulouria* – those rolls like quoits with sesame? – on the streets all day. My mother did cleaning, sewing, washing for rich women, to feed us all. But we were starving.'

'Can you remember so far back?'

'Of course. Everything. One night I remember my mother was mending by the kerosene lamp in the warehouse we were living in, in Thessaloniki. My grandmother put her hand on her shoulder.

' "Melpo," she said. "It is time you thought of

yourself."

'My mother lifted her red eyes but said nothing.

' "You are young. Your whole life is ahead of you. And what about your children?"

' "Mama," my mother answered. "Don't say this."

' "It is what I would do. He is my own son, my only son. But it is what you will have to do sooner or later. He will manage somehow, he is a man. Think of yourself as a widow, Melpo. The War will go on for years. You are still beautiful. There are good men who will help you. It is not a sin. You have no money, no home, no food. I mean what I am saying."

' "No. Your son believes in me and I have always deserved it. I always will."

'Yiayia shook her scarved head and said nothing more. Her eyelids were wet. My mother went on sewing. My baby brother cried out and I rocked and hushed him back to sleep. When I looked back, my mother was still and sagging over her work, so Yiayia took it away and laid her down to sleep and pulled the flour sack over her. She saw me watching, and hugged me.

' "*Aman, paidaki mou*," she wailed, but quietly. "You must be the man of the family now."

' "I know, Yiayia," I said. "I am already." '

He lies still. Kerry bends over and kisses his brown forehead. 'I'm nervous,' she says again. Her long soft breasts nudge his ears. He feels her shiver. The gold spokes of sun have gone out of the water, leaving it black.

'Don't be.'

'Have we known each other long enough? Can we be sure? Long enough to get married?'

'Well, let me see. How long is it?'

'Ten months. No, eleven.'

'Is it eleven months?' He smiles. 'That sounds enough.'

'What will your mother think?'

'That we should wait. But I don't want to. You don't, do you?'

'No. She might like me, you never know.'

'Yes. Don't be too hard on her, will you, if she is rude?

And by the way, better don't wear pants.'

'Pardon?'

'Pants. Trousers? Overalls? "Womans should wear only dresses." '

'Oh God!'

'It is her old age.'

'I don't have a dress. Or a skirt. I don't *own* one.'

'Oh. Well, never mind. Don't look like that. No, listen.' He sits up, agitated. 'Forget I said it. She can hardly see. Glaucoma.'

'What flowers does she like?'

'Oh, anything.'

'Roses?'

'Yes. Fine.'

'Oh God! I hope we come through this!'

'Darling, of course we will.'

'Do you love me?'

'Yes, of course. *Kouragio!*'

She grins back at him, pushing her fingers through the shaggy grey curls at his temples. Shadow lies all over the bay and the far city. High above, a gull hangs and sways, silent, its red legs folded, still deeply sunlit.

                                        *

Eleni and Voula, exchanging looks, have served Kerry iced water, a dish of tough green figs in syrup, a glass of Marsala, then Turkish coffee. They have exclaimed over her roses and argued amiably about vases. Flustered, Kerry waits, avoiding Jimmy's eyes. She feels gruff and uncouth, awkward. A bell rings three times in another room. '*Pane*, Dimitri,' Eleni hisses. Jimmy bounds away. Kerry grins blindly at the sisters.

When he comes back and leads her to his mother's room, hot behind brown blinds and stinking of disinfectant, she misses the old woman at first among the jumbled laces and tapestries, the grey and golden faces under glass: a skull on a lace pillow, mottled, and tufted with white down. Only her thick eyes move, red-rimmed, loose in their pleated lids.

'Dimitri?' The voice a hoarse chirrup. 'This is Keri?'

'Kerry, yes. I'm glad to meet you, Mrs Yanna-kopoulou.'

'Good. Thank you for the roses.' Rumpled already, they sag in dim porcelain, mirrored. '*Keri* is candle in our language. *Keri* is wox.'

'Wax, Mama.'

'Yairs. Wox for candle. Dimitri, *agori mou*, put the lamp, I carn see Keri. Now leave us alone. We tok woman to woman.'

The door closes. Yellow folds of her cheeks move. She is slowly smiling.

'*Katse*, Keri, siddown.' Kerry sits in the cane armchair by the bed. 'My daughters they tell me about you.'

'They're very nice.'

'Yairs. They like you. They say good thinks about you. She hev a good heart, this *filenada* of Dzimmy, they say. She love him too much. She good mother for her little boy. Where your husband is, Keri?'

'My ex-husband. In Queensland, as far as I know. We aren't in touch.'

'Why he leave you? He hev another womans?'

'I don't know. He's been gone years.'

'You doan know?'

'No, Mrs Yannakopoulou.'

'You were very yunk.'

'Twenty-two. My son is nine.'

'How old you say?'

'Nine. *Ennea*.'

'Ach! You speak Greek!'

'I'm learning.'

'Yairs. Is very hard lenguage. How old you are, Keri?'

'Thirty.'

'Thirty. Yairs. You too old to learn Greek.'

'Oh, I'll manage. *Echo kouragio*.'

'*Kouragio!* Ah bravo.' A giggle shakes the bedcovers. 'Good. You will need *thet*, if you love Dimitri. He is quiet man. Mysterious. Always he joke. You will need to be stronk. You are, yairs. Not *oraia*, that doesun mutter.

How you say?'

'*Oraia*? Beautiful. I know I'm not.'

'Better not. You not uckly. Too *oraia* no good. They fall in love with they own faces. They mek the men jealoust.' A smile bares the wires around her loose eye-teeth. 'Lonk time now Dimitri tellink me: this woman, this Keri, Mama, I want you to meet her. Keri? I say. Her name Kyriaki? No, he say, she Australian woman, she not Greek. Not Greek, Dimitri? I doan want to meet her. But he keep saying please, Mama. Orright, I say. If you thinkink to merry her, orright. Because now I hev not lonk time to live.'

'Oh, Mrs Yannakopoulou – '

'Orright. Is not secret. Everybody know.' Her hand clamps Kerry's arm. 'And before I go on my lonk, my eternity trip, I want to see my boy heppy. That is all I want now. My boy to be heppy.'

'Yes, well – '

'You are also mother. You hev a mother heart. You want what is best for your boy. You do anythink for him?'

'Yes, but – '

'You good woman. Good-heart woman. You hev *kouragio*. So mek me one favour. For *my* boy.'

'What?'

'Tell Dimitri you woan merry him. You love him. Orright. I understend love. Love him. Look after him. Live with him, orright. *Aman*. Doan merry him.'

Kerry pulls her arm away. The lamp casts a wet light on the ravelled cheeks and throat.

'So I'm not good enough.'

'You *good*. I doan say thet. But divorce woman. Not for Dimitri, no. Not for merry.'

'But he's divorced!'

'Doesun mutter. Is different. She *putana*, thet woman. He love her too much, but she go with our neighbour, our enemy. Is shame for all our femily. We come to Australia for new life. Is not Dimitri fault.'

'Yes, I know. He told me.'

'Hwat he tell you?'

'It was twenty *years* ago.'

'His heart *break*. Some children they find them one night together in the pear orchard: Magda with our enemy. They mother tell me. Dimitri was away. When Magda come home, I tok to her, I tell her I know, all the village know. I cry for my poor son. He will kill you, I say. She cry, she scream. She say she waitink baby. I say we want no *bastardo* in our femily. I pack all her *proika*. I say, go and never come back. When he come home, *I* tell Dimitri.'

The scaled eyes close, wet-rimmed. Kerry sighs.

'He told me about it. My divorce wasn't my fault either. And I don't play around.'

'For Dimitri next time should be only *parthena*. Veergin.'

'Isn't that up to Dimitri?'

'Is up to *you* now. You know thet, Keri. You can say no. Say *wait*.'

'And then what?'

'I know Greek girls of good femilies – '

'No. You tried that before. He told me. He wasn't interested, was he? Why arrange a marriage these days? I love Jimmy. We want to get married fairly soon. I'm going to have a baby. Jimmy's baby.'

'Hwat? You waitink baby?'

'Yes.'

'Hwen?'

'August.'

'August. I understend now.'

'So you see – '

'You should be *shame*!'

'Ashamed of a baby? Why, what's wrong with it? We aren't living in the Dark Ages. Jimmy's very happy. He likes kids. Ben adores him. He'll be a good father.'

'I understend now why he want to merry you. *Apo filotimo!* For honour. Because you trick him.'

'No. That isn't true.'

'You know hwat womans can do if they doan want

baby. You know.'

'I *do* want the baby. So does he. You have no right – '

'I hev the right of mother. The right of mother who will die soon! My only livink son! Doan break my heart!'

Kerry, her face hot, pats the writhing yellow hands and stands up.

'I'd better go, Mrs Yannakopoulou. I'm sorry.'

'Wait! Listen to me: I hev money. Yes, I hev. They doan know nothink. Inside the bed.' She claws at the mattress. 'Gold pounds! Hwere they are? Take them. Hev the baby. Leave Dimitri alone. Hwere they are?'

'No, thanks.' Kerry pulls a wry face. 'I'm sorry about all this. And I was hoping you'd like me.'

The old woman is moaning. Her eyes and mouth clamp shut, and she starts shaking. Kerry shuts the door softly on the dense lamplight and goes on tiptoe to the kitchen. It is full of shrill chatter. Saucepans hiss, bouncing their lids, gushing sunlit steam. All over the table sprawl glowing red and green peppers ready to be stuffed. Jimmy, Eleni, Voula, and three children, all suddenly silent, stare with identical eyes like dates; stare up in alarm.

'Someone better go to her. Quickly.'

The sisters hurry off.

'Darling, what's wrong? What happened?'

'Ask your mother. Can you take me home?'

'Of course. Just let's wait till she – '

'It's all right, I'll get a tram. Will you come round later, though, please?'

'Yes, of course. Unless she – '

'Look, if it's all off, fair enough. But you're not to punish me. I *wasn't* hard on her.'

'Oh, Kerry, punish? Why would it be all off?'

The children are gazing open-mouthed.

'She'll tell you.'

'You tell me.'

Kerry shakes her head, reddening.

'You are punishing *me*! Why are you angry?'

'Oh, later!'

The bell rings three times. Jimmy bounds down the passage.

'Mama?' His voice breaks. 'Mama?'

'Leave me alone, all of you. And you, go with your *putana*. Leave me alone.' She struggles to turn to the shadowed wall. '*To fos. Kleis' to fos.*'

He turns off the lamp and ushers his sisters out, though they linger, he knows, whispering behind the door.

'She had to go home.'

'Good!'

'*Min klais, Mamaka.*' He smooths her sodden hair. 'No, Don't cry. Don't cry. No. No.'

'Give me a tablet. No, this ones. Water.' He slips his arm behind her knobbled back as she gulps, flinching. 'Ach. *Pikro einai.* Bitter.'

'Tell me what happened.'

But she is silent. He picks up the photograph on her dresser. It is one of the last photographs of his father. His father is sitting in the doorway, feeding Eleni's two little daughters spoonfuls of bread-and-milk. They coaxed him in baby talk for *paparitsa*. It was his *paparitsa*, not theirs. It was all he could eat by then. A white hen is tiptoeing past them. Wheat was heaped in the long room that year, a great trickling tawny mountain; the barn was too full already of barley and sesame. The best harvest since the War, his father said. Bravo, Dimitri. None of them has seen the hen yet. In the light at the door they are like three shadow puppets on a screen. He alone looks frayed, dim, melting in the air. His death is near. He regrets, Dimitri thinks, that I have had no children. No grandchild of my sowing, no grandson to bear his name. Still, he is smiling.

In the photograph the bread-and-milk bowl is white. In fact it was butter yellow and, catching the light, glowed in his father's hands like a harvest moon.

'Mama?' he says softly.

'*Nai.*'

'Tell me what happened.'

'She can tell you.'

'*Ela. Pes mou.*'

'This Keri. She hev not the right name. She not wox. Wox? She stone. Iron.'

'Why?'

'You want *her?* Hwat for? She not yunk. Not *oraia.* Not Greek. Not rich. For *proika* she hev hwat? A boy. A big boy. She zmok.'

'No.' He grins. 'She doesn't.'

'Australian womans they all zmok. Puff poof. Puff poof.'

'Kerry doesn't.'

'Dimitraki, listen to me. I know you like I know my hand. You my son. You doan love Keri.' She hesitates, then dares: 'Not like you love Magda.'

'Leave Magda out of it.'

'Thet time I save you.'

'Magda is gone. I was too young then. Forget Magda. I love Kerry now.'

'She waitink baby.'

'Yes.'

'Why you doan tok? You should be tell me this, not Keri. Is too big shock.' She sighs. 'If is your baby.'

'It is.'

'How you know? She maybe trick you. Australian womans –'

'Mama, I know.'

'*How* you know? Divorce woman!'

'Mama, I love Kerry. I trust Kerry. I need Kerry. All right?'

'*Thet* is how?' He is silent. 'You engry?'

'No.'

'Yes. You engry with me.'

'No. You will see in August if it is or not.'

'*Aman*, Dimitri,' she moans.

'Enough, Mama, now.'

'Orright, enough. Enough. Merry her, then. I am too tired for fight. Do hwat you want. But you wronk, you know?'

He waits.

'I hope so she hev a boy. For the name, your Baba name. Is good for his name to live. August, *aman*! You think I livink thet long, to see your little boy?'

'Mama, you will.' He squeezes her hand. 'My little girl, maybe. My little Melpo.'

'*Ochi*. If is girl, I doan want the name Melpo.'

'Kerry does.'

'Tell Keri if is girl, she must not call her Melpo.'

'You tell her. Next time she comes.'

'I *never* see her again.'

'Ah, Mamaka.'

'No. Sometime you askink *too* much.'

'You know,' he sighs, 'that if I have a girl, I will call her Melpo.'

'I doan want you to!'

'You do so.'

'*Aman*, Dimitri *mou*. Put me *rodostamo*.'

He tips red rosewater into his palm and sits stroking it over her cheeks and forehead and whimpering throat, the thin loose spotted skin of her forearms.

'Her heart is stone.'

'No. She is strong. Like you, she has had to be.'

'She will control your life, you want thet?'

'I *think* I can get used to it.'

'Well. I done my best. I hope so you woan be sorry, you know?'

'Thank you, Mama.'

He bends and kisses her ruffled cheek. Her eyes close.

'*Ela pio konta*,' She whispers. 'Closer. I have gold pounds inside the bed. Your Aunt Sophia's. Ach, if I had them in the War! The baby died from hunger. Take them, *paidi mou*. Doan tell the girls. Take them for your baby.'

'*Aman*, Mama. You and your gold pounds. You gave them to Magda. You drove her away. And I forgave you. Remember?'

'For your good. For honour.'

But only after years, Mama, he thinks. Bitter years.

'Sleep,' he says.

'I carn. I pain too much. Go and tell Eleni to come. Bring a clean sheet, tell her. When she goes, come back. Sit with me.'

'Can I do anything?'

'Nothink. Maybe Keri waitink you?'

'She will understand.'

'No. Go to her. When I was yunk, I was stronk. My God. Remember? And *oraia* also.'

'I know. There was not a woman like you in all Makedonia. You had a spirit like fire.'

'Hold my hend, Dimitri.'

One day when you are not tired, Mama, he thinks, I must ask you: do you remember the storm, that last summer in the village, before the War when I was five? You sat on the porch in this cane armchair suckling Eleni. The rain was a grey wall. Hens shot past us slithering in the brown mud. The clouds were slashed by lightning and by spokes of sunlight. Afterwards I led the horse out, fighting to hold his head down, but he tore at the grapevine, splashing rain in clusters on us all. White-eyed, his dark silver hide shivering, he munched vine leaves. I was angry. You laughed so much, Eleni lost your nipple, and kicked and wailed. Then I laughed too.

Remember how we stood in the river thigh-deep, slipping on bronze rocks. You taught me to catch little fish in my hands. We threaded them on the green stalks of water plants.

SALLY'S BIRTHDAY

The pub the same as ever, good old pub. The same rippled green glass in its diamond windows, the hot bread reek of beer, and nests of smoke fuzzing the thick lamps day and night. Lamplight on the rough glass flickers like glowing leaves. No trees out there, though. Warehouses, and a few shops, factories. The faces under the lamps are red, shiny with sweat. No one is staring at him. Here it's live and let live. He smacks his glass down.

'Another beer, Mike.'

'Fair go, matey. Where's the fire?'

'Daughter's birthday today. Celebrating. Go on, have a heart.'

'Want to get me into trouble, do you?'

'Come and sit here, dear. Have one with me. Two pots, Mike.'

A roll-necked redhead further along the bar is beaming and nodding, waggling a fat hand with rings on. He moves down. The barman shrugs.

'Go for your lives.'

'Oh, thanks, Mike. Keep the change.'

'Well, thank you, missus. Cheers. Daughter's birthday today.'

'Is it, love? Well, now. How old's your daughter?'

Good question.

'Twenty-one. She's twenty-one today.'

'Well, here's wishing your daugher very many happies. What's her name, darling?'

'Sally.' He sucks a long cold draught. 'Sally.'

'Happy birthday to Sally. Sally Kelly with a rope round her neck.'

'Sally Jones.'

The woman wipes froth off her chin. She sighs and sips more.

'Haven't seen her for donkeys' years. Not since the old Yallourn days. She was going on seven.'

'How come, dear?'

'Her mother took off with her. We'd had a bad blue. Ended up here in Melbourne. She had a sister here. I didn't know where they were. Got a postcard one day. No address. Just "Meet us at the coffee lounge at five on March the tenth. Sally wants to see you."'

'That's today.'

'Sally's birthday, see.'

'Oh yes, Sally's birthday. Well, here's to Sally. Married again, did you, dear?'

'Me? Shit no. Once is enough.'

'Go on. You never know.'

'I bloody know.'

'Ah,' she sighs again. 'Ah well.' There are tears in her eyes. 'That's life, isn't it? That's life for you.'

*

He was waiting in the coffee lounge by half past four, though she'd said five in her postcard. By the window so he could see them coming, Jan with Sally, on her seventh birthday. He was afraid that Sally might not know him. His own face looked strange to him gazing in the plate glass, blue-lit; all the other faces that came and went further inside were gold, in a haze of steam, ribboned with smoke. Six o'clock. He had his presents and the cake wrapped on the seat beside him, and a big blonde sleeping doll in cellophane that the girls in the canteen had put in for. It was the right coffee lounge. The one she'd worked in, they always went there.

The street became dark, and his face too turned dim gold. He was on his fifth coffee. It rained, and stopped raining, and started again. Seven o'clock. Cars sprayed veils of rain under the streetlamps. Strangers splashed past. The lamps in the coffee lounge hung behind his head, huge luminous orange balls, juggled and frozen there.

It was the right coffee lounge.

At eight o'clock he got up and without a glance at the things on the seat walked out.

*

'Do you have a good cognac? Courvoisier? A Napoleon brandy?'

'No, miss, sorry. Nothing like that.'

She is tall, sleekly dressed in black velvet. Her hair is in short black curls like an astrakhan cap. Green eyes slope upward in her white face. Sally in that last photo had her hair like that. Green eyes, too. The image of Sally.

'Come on. Give young lady whatever she's after. Hear me?' They all stare in the bottle shop as he leans over the counter. 'Go ahead, mate. Give lady what she wants.' But they ignore him.

'This is the only brandy I got in stock, miss.'

'Oh, well, that'll do, thanks.' She sighs, pays for it and hugging the bottle in its brown bag steps into the street. Headlights glow over her.

'Miss, mind if I ask your name?'

'Yes, I do, actually.'

'Got a good reason.'

People are looking. She hesitates.

'Please. I got a good reason. For asking.'

She stares as he shivers in front of her, wringing his wet hairy hands.

'Marian,' she says. She hurries across with the green light.

Marian? Not Sally? Not Sally?

*

Following her at a cunning distance, he loses her long black shape again and again in dimly lamplit streets, but sees her at last open a wooden door with stained-glass tulips in it. Beyond a tiled verandah and low fence and gate. He knocks. His words tangle, explaining to the hostile round blur of her face. Sally, it's your Dad. Your old Dad. Sally! He sees her go watery, then dark, dark, and falls at her feet in a dead faint.

*

A white dog, long and supple as a fawn, breathing and licking in front of a log fire, looks up grinning.

I feel crook, Sally. Where are you? Sally, I feel crook. The dog pants. No other sound. He sleeps.

*

He dreams he is looking for Sally in a wild green sea. He rises and sinks in terror. At last he sees her in the distance, a little girl crouched in a snowy plain lost in an immense grey twilight. Cold falls through the air. She is burning matches to set fire to her body. Luminous flames batter against her. Dying away they leave a heap of ashes in a hole of sodden yellow grass. The wind swerves and roars. There is nothing in any direction but barren snow.

*

When he wakes again he is snotty with tears. He keeps his eyes shut. He assumes this is another morning in Pedro's room. Good old Pedro the Dago, his best mate all those years up north, ever since Groote Eylandt. Quiet as a mouse, the old Pedro, sitting in corners with his guitar, until he got hold of some grog, then he'd go wild and fire shots in the air, chuck empties at anything that moved, and howl and scream and swear. Listen to who's talking. All right, but I draw the line at shooting, mate. Well, he could always have a kip on the camp bed at Pedro's, and bugger the landlady. On one wall there is a long lady in charcoal, twice life-size, and from time to time Pedro has added hairs in pencil, and moles, and tattoos. Squatting in front of her. She has huge tits and hips. Her name Conchita, Pedro said. She a big whore, mate. You can call her Connie. She was there when Pedro took the room, part of the furniture, but he's done a lot to her since. Pedro has never said who Conchita was. He himself has never mentioned Jan. He looks up now

with a shy grin for Pedro, but this is not Pedro's room.
Pedro? he croaks. He could have sworn. But he is too
exhausted to insist.

*

A long white dog lying with its head on its paws looks
up, yawns, and wanders back to the fire. There is no
lamp, only this golden ebb and flow of rustling light. In
the warmth of it his clothes stink, sour and musty. He is
embarrassed by his singlet and shirt stiff with sweat, and
the lumber jacket, its seams ripped now, borrowed from
Pedro three weeks ago. Never needed this much clobber
up north, Pedro, eh. His shoes are battered and grey. So,
when he checks it in the round mirror over the fireplace,
is his face. The grey bristles of his hair and whiskers are
clumped around scabs.

The dog sniffs him. Good dog. Good boy.

On the mantelpiece a bottle of dark green glass sits
with a candle in its mouth. CHAMPAGNE COGNAC, he
spells out. The glass is dim, like fragments found on
beaches, their sharp glitter worn and blinded by years in
sea water. He picks it up. Trickles of wax like white roots
cling round it. He gives it a shake, and wax falls in the
fire. He peers into it against the firelight. Not a drop.

'Are you feeling better?'

Never laid eyes on this one in his life.

'Er, yeah. Thanks a lot. Er.'

'Would you like a cup of coffee? No? Tea?'

'Er, well, tea'd be beaut, thanks, miss.'

'Milk? Sugar?'

'No milk. Two sugar. Thanks. Er, miss? How come
I –'

Baffled, he waves his shabby arms.

'You passed out on my doorstep.'

'Shit, did I? Jeeze. I'm sorry about that. Makes you the
Good Samaritan, eh.'

She grins back, shrugs, and disappears. He remembers
a pub with lamps in the afternoon. It is already night,
though, at these firelit windows. In the pub some fat old

redhead bought him a beer. A birthday. Whose, hers? That bit about the Good Samaritan was a bloody inspiration. Made quite an impression, knowing something from the Bible. More than just some old derro. Hidden depths. Course, it helps a lot to have a way with people. I always did have a way with people. They always want to look after me. The sheilas especially. All except Jan, the bitch. Funny that. Like that waitress in where was it? Gympie. Wanted to get married. I love you, Larry. Love you, love you so much. Oh God. Don't ever leave me, Larry. Oh darling.

'Here's your tea.'

Lovely voice this one's got. Like Pedro's guitar.

'Oh, ta, miss.'

He stirs it and sips, burning his cracked lips. She is kneeling to stroke her dog. He pats it. It looks sidelong at him. On its bent haunches the white hide is crisp as a calf's.

'Nice dog you got there. What's his name?'

'Bianca. It's a she.'

'Big, isn't she?'

'She's only a baby yet. What's your name?'

'Told you, didn't I?'

'No. I don't think so.'

'Larry Jones.' He stares across the dog at her dark curling hair. Now he remembers. He knows who she is.

'Mine's Marian.'

'That's funny,' he says. 'Marian. What's your Mum's name?'

'Sylvie.'

'Sylvie, eh? That's funny.'

'She's French.'

'No. No. You look like someone.'

'Do I?'

'You look like my daughter. The spitting image of her.'

'Really? What's her name?'

'Sally.' He leans forward. 'I bet it's your birthday today.'

'No. Why?'

'It's Sally's.' He blows on the tea and sips some. 'It's her twenty-first.'

'Oh, really? Is she having a party?'

'I wouldn't know. They say she's dead.'

'What!'

'That's what they reckon. Inform, I should say. That's how you find out these things, see. Like when the wife got her divorce and got married again. Letter from the lawyer bloke. Dear Mr Jones, we have been instructed by our client, Mrs Janet Thompson, to inform you that blah blah.'

'How did she die?'

'Drowned. Down Apollo Bay way. Kennett River. Ever been there? Last summer.'

'Oh, how terrible! I'm sorry.'

'I hadn't seen her for a long time. I mean fourteen years is a bloody long time. If it's true, my Sally's been dead for months.' He stares into the flowing red and gold of the splintered logs. 'If it's not, I'd know her. If I see her again, I'll know her.'

*

We have been instructed by our client, Mrs Janet Thompson, to inform you that your daughter, Sarah Margaret Thompson, drowned on 17 February this year while swimming in heavy surf at Kennett River, Victoria. Miss Thompson's body was recovered, but all attempts to revive her were unsuccessful. A funeral service for Miss Thompson was held at the Memorial Park Crematorium, Altona, on 21 February. May we extend our deepest sympathy to you in your loss.

*

That's how it went, something like that. He glances up from the fire. She is staring at him. As if she's seen a ghost. Maybe she has.

'They changed her name,' he explains, 'soon as her Mum got married again. To a respectable bloke. It was me Sally wanted to live with. Steal me, Daddy! she says. We'll run away and live together, you and me. No fear, I says. Want your Dad to end up in jail? I been sorry ever since. Let her down, see. Her Dad never let her down before. Deserved to lose her, eh. And I done time inside anyway. I was inside when the letter came. Only got out last month. Tell you what. It's not that bad. Life goes on.'

'Why would they make up a story like that?'

'If you knew her Mum,' he snorted, 'you wouldn't ask.'

'You can check with the Registrar of Births, Deaths and Marriages.'

'Oh, I will, don't worry. They can't keep me in the dark forever.'

A great joy has begun to burn in him. He sucks the last cold drop of tea and puts his cup down. Clumsily. It falls and rolls on the saucer, spilling sandy sugar. She stands up.

'Are you feeling better?'

'Bit better now, thanks, love.'

'Could you eat something?'

'No. No. Couldn't keep it down.'

'You're sure you'll be all right?'

'Bit of a snooze and I'll be right as rain. If that's all right, miss. If I'm not in the way.'

'Well. All right then. I'll leave you to it.'

'Wait on.' She is letting him stay! He feels in his torn pockets. 'Got a photo here. Last one she sent. Used to write to me now and then. Send photos. They always caught up with me sooner or later. Somewhere up north.'

It has cracked and faded: a glossy print of a smiling schoolgirl with crinkled dark hair. It is inscribed on the back. *From Sally, with love to my Dad. X O*

He waits as she looks intently as if into a mirror.

'So what if they changed her name,' he says, taking his time. 'Sally'll still know I'm her real Dad.'

*

At Cowes that last summer, the time they were boarding at a guest house, Sally came fishing off the pier at daybreak. She made such a song and dance about it that he took her. He woke her at five. They walked hand in hand down streets still sunken in cool darkness, their footsteps chiming against the black plate glass. Wisps of cloud turned pink, then gold. He cast again and again, catching nothing. A seal looping in the green water below gazed as she knelt calling. Daddy, look. It likes me. Catch it for me.

Oh Sally love.

*

Flames in glass flutter and breathe. The dog whines, nosing at its singed hide, it is so close to the fire. There is a rug over him now: he jumps up with a cry, then sits down slowly, dizzy, sick. Take it easy now. Where the fuck? Oh, Sally's place. Lie down and listen to voices muttering. Whose?

Somewhere in another room, her voice and a bloke's. One, then the other. Her voice a slow guitar, then the bloke's threatening, it sounds like, annoyed, but finally laughing, convinced, or distracted. Now both are silent. He lies in a sweat. Bloke's not going to mind if her old Dad stays the night, is he? Don't say Sally's married. All these years and it seems only yesterday.

By the time the lawyer's letter caught up with him it was July or August and if it was true she'd long been incinerated by then. Her hair, her white flesh burned. Shards of bone left, bones and ash. Ashen bones. A lock of hair she had sent him, all that was left, he had gone and lost God only knew where, once when he was drunk and disorderly and woke with a blank mind in Darwin jail. His last letter came back from the lawyer's: *Sally love, this is a view of Ayers Rock. I promise I'll come down south and see you soon as I can. Your loving Dad. X O*

His bladder will burst. Where's the bloody john? He creeps unsteadily through the firelight with the slender dog smiling and nudging him through the archway where she had appeared, hadn't she? Yes, with the tea. A throbbing pale refrigerator, a dark grey sink. The deep house lying in wait. He huddles over the sink, groping through layers of clothes. The piss splashes and rebounds in a loud spray. He struggles with a tap. Too tight.

Oh Jesus Christ.

Still in the paper bag, her bottle of brandy that she was buying when he saw her: sitting there on the table. And if that's not Fate, I don't know what is. Grabbing it, he stumbles back to the firelight. Slumps on the couch. Pulls the rug up over his thudding head. At long last he manages to twist the cork out and have one long hot swig. Happy birthday, Sally. And another.

*

The door slamming startles him awake. A car starts up. Headlights, sweeping over the pane through thin curtains, flash over the room. The fire is dying. Sally? he croaks.

'Oh! Are you all right?'

'Sally. Come here a minute. Want a word with you.'

'It's Marian.'

'Don't give a fuck! You can call yourself Cinderella! Anyone can change their fucking name!'

She snaps the light on and gasps at the sight of him wildly grinning up, the bottle in its soggy bag clutched to his chest.

'Have some.'

'No, thank you.'

'Celebrating. You never told me you were married.'

'I'm divorced.'

'Oh. Who's the bloke, then?'

'He's a friend of mine.'

'Don't give me that. It's your Dad here, remember? And I've seen it all. Friend going to marry you, is he?'

'It's not really your business.'

'Turn light off.'

'He's coming back.'

'Turn fucking light off!'

Soft darkness covers the room. His stung eyes can open.

'What's time?'

'Half past twelve.'

'Divorced, eh? She's done a good job. Here's to your mother.' He has a sip. 'Friend going to marry you, is he, Sally?'

'He's married.'

'I see. Well, well. Gone home to his wife.'

'Can I get you anything? You look terrible.'

He lifts the bottle for another swig, but this burning in his belly will be the death of him. He groans.

'No. Want to talk.'

'Let me just get –'

'Sit down!'

She squats to stir the embers in the grate, and is outlined with fire. The dog whimpers, its long head laid in her lap.

'Don't hold yourself cheap.'

She nods.

'Hear me? Don't hold yourself cheap.'

She nods, her back still turned.

'Any bloke'll have a bit if you rub his nose in it. Hop in for his chop. Too right. Be a fool not to. Then you're the whore for letting him. See? Your mother might have got away with it. Your mother was a rotten lying whore. She'll burn in hell for it. You're not like that, are you, Sally?'

She stands looking down at him.

'You've turned out a very lovely young woman. Man can be proud of you.'

That gets a smile out of her.

'Voice like a guitar.'

'Oh, come on!'

'No bloke's going to think he can treat my daughter like a whore. I'll soon piss the bastard off.'

She laughs. He joins in with a joyous cackle.

'That's the way. That's my girl. Piss him off, eh? Get me a drink of water, will you, love? Feel a bit crook.'

She hurries through the archway. The light snaps on. He wasn't too harsh, was he? A Dad's got a duty, like it or not. Then he hears her sniff and gasp. He remembers. With a moan he remembers groping in the dark. Pissing in her bloody sink. Oh Jesus Christ. A torrent of water gushes in the sink. Stronger hands than me. He squeezes his eyes shut and huddles down. Oh God, Sally, he rehearses silently, I'm real crook, love. I'm dying, Sally.

'Here's your water.'

'Ah.' He gulps some. 'Thanks, love. I'm crook, Sally.'

'Where do you live? They'll be worried about you.'

'Got this mate in Punt Road. Pedro. Pedro the Dago. What his mates call him.'

'That's miles away. This is Carlton.'

'Carlton, eh?'

'Can I give him a ring to come and get you?'

'Not on the phone, love. He won't worry, though. Shit no. He's prob'ly gone fishing.' A quick sip of the water, a grin. 'Hey, remember that last holiday at Cowes? Trooping through those tunnels in the tea-tree, remember? The sand was like fire. We could hear the sea a mile off, and cicadas. We went fishing. I was teaching you to swim, Sally.'

She stands up. His eyes are sore. He shuts them.

'What did you say?'

'I was teaching you to swim.'

'Where in Punt Road?' Her voice is far-off, and tense. 'Will I ring a taxi for you?'

She is holding the front door open.

'Hold your horses. What's going on?'

'I'm sorry. I must ask you to go now.'

'What do you mean, you're sorry? Kicking me out?'

'Please, just go.'

'What did I do?'

'Never mind.'

'We got to have a talk! It's important!'

'No, I'm sorry.'

'What do you mean, I'm sorry?'

'I'm sorry, but you have to go.'

'Well I like that. Middle of the fucking night. My own fucking daughter. If I'm not disappointed in you!'

'Come on, please.'

'Just a minute.' He is on his weaving feet. He peers at her. 'Hang on. Give us a good look. You look like Sally all right. But I don't think you *are*.'

He only waves the bottle to emphasize the outrage of it, but she recoils and shrieks. The white dog cringes.

'Get *out*!'

As he wavers, intent on remonstrating, she gives him a wild push that sends him staggering, gaping, out on to the verandah. The door slams. Lights flash on in all her windows. Silence.

'Sorry won't mend it,' he grumbles. Whore.

*

He hugs the bottle in the bag, wandering down a street filled with flurries of light. Lamps and housefronts and footpaths shimmer as if behind flawed glass or in the shaken air above a fire. Then there is the moon, sitting full and golden on the roof of the brewery. It is still there when he blinks. A fiery blur.

Across the glinting tramlines, if only he can make it, is the old pub.

With caution he starts out, eyeing his shadow on the wet bitumen, lights flaring under his feet, across tram rails and then more rails. Make it. You can make it. Rails surge round his feet. Cars slide past and daze him. It is too small for a pub. It has a tower, seats, diamond windows. A sign. He spells it out LADIES.

Propped against its dank wall he fumbles at the bottle, but it slithers out of his hands and cracks with a fat splash at his feet. He sinks down, scrabbling in wet paper and broken moonlit glass. He sucks salt blood and brandy off his fingers. Glass stings his lip. Tears spill down his face, through his nose, out of his jagged mouth.

Oh Sally love. I'm sorry.

*

In his dream he is rising again, bobbing and stumbling, stunned, deafened, hurtled, out of a shaggy uproar of green waves. He is carrying to safety his lost, his only daughter. Cicadas rasp. Her eyes open and smile at him. He lays her gently on the sand.

SAINT KAY'S DAY

How warm even a cold white room became when you turned on the light! Any light would do the trick. Candlelight was best of all, though, with its little shadowy fires. And a room that faced the sunset was like a cave behind a waterfall, when you lit candles in it and made shadows arch their wings like bats on its walls and ceiling. With the shutters closed you could be anywhere in the world. With them open, you were in Greece: over the balcony rail was Mount Olympus, printed indigo on the hot sky, and all the still gulf in between had little boats pulling threads in the silk of it. What did it matter if the room that faced the sunset was the only room you had, except of course for a narrow kitchen, and a dark bathroom no bigger than a telephone box? (And if little pale celluloid cockroaches scurried into the air vent whenever you switched the light on in that bathroom.) Even if the power did keep failing. And her flat was small and dark and so icy – and this was only November, late November – that she ached and shuddered all day.

Sunset was when the lizard crept out and spread his sleek bronze skin on the warm glow of one wall. He was company, the rippling lizard.

'Aren't you lonely there, Kay?' Letters from home kept asking that. 'When are you coming home? What's Thessaloniki got that Sydney hasn't?'

Thessaloniki has Aleko, her letters never said in reply: Aleko was still too new. Besides, was it only Aleko?

'We miss you, you know,' pleaded the letters.

'Well, I miss you,' she wrote back. 'But Thessaloniki is

very beautiful and strange. More than Athens even. I've hardly begun to see the real Thessaloniki.'

'We're not getting any younger as you know.' Her father wrote as he spoke, flatly. 'Your Mum and I were hoping you'd be back this Christmas. First it was "my studies". Now it's "my working holiday". That's all very well, but you have to settle down sometime, don't you.'

'I've taken on students for English lessons. I can't let them down and just leave, can I?'

'But *aren't* you lonely, dear?' That was her mother.

'Well, you see, there's this lizard,' she wrote, 'and a sweet little Burmese cat . . .' The letters ignored that.

It *was* sweet, a spoilt coquette of a little cat, in this city of starved strays too. It came faithfully to her door every day after the siesta for its plate of warm milk. When she stroked it, it closed its eyes in its bat-eared black face and stretched itself in poses of pure lust. Its deep-furred bony little body vibrated warmly; it was just beautiful. It gave her hope that her own bony body would, when – *if* – the time came, be beautiful for Aleko. She told Aleko, in Greek, that she loved the cat because it spoke English: just as she hoped, he laughed aloud. He was at his most handsome then. His mouth, widening, lost its petulant droop. Because there was something petulant and spoilt about Aleko at times. He *was* selfish, he was vain. But he would grow out of it. He had a kind heart. Once he asked, looking down, looking at her hands as thin as dry leaves on the table: 'Why you are alone in your life, Kay?' So she told him about the man in Australia that she had loved and never really got over . . .

'It spik Greek too, this clever cat,' spluttered Aleko, in English. 'Ask it if it spik Burmese!' And, why she didn't know, but they collapsed at this and laughed together till they cried.

Aleko came for a lesson twice a week at around sunset. He always stayed on, though, drinking coffee in her chilly kitchen long after the hour was up. She was always free: in her two months in Thessaloniki Aleko was the only student she had found. The sixty drachmas that he paid her twice a week covered the rent; that was only five hundred a month. For everthing else but the rent she had to withdraw savings. Any day now she hoped to find more students: it was hard without a telephone or a work permit. Her notices in English in the two libraries were still up:

ENGLISHWOMAN (because no one wanted an Australian accent): M.A. GRADUATE: SEEKS ADULT STUDENTS FOR ENGLISH LESSONS IN YOUR OWN HOME: 60 DRACHMAS PER HOUR (and her name and her address).

Aleko came to her place, his had no privacy. Aleko had written out notices in Greek for her. He might know someone who wanted lessons, or so he had hinted. He enjoyed hinting.

'Is your name's day next Thursday, you know thet,' he said after the last lesson, when they were waiting for the lift. 'We hev little party, okay, Kay? I bring a cake.'

'*My* name's day? Saint *Kay*?'

'Agia Aikaterini. Is the same. Aikaterini, Katerina, Katy, Kay.' With a quick smile as the lift bumped and opened: 'We be hev good time. Okay? Kay?' It amused him to say that.

'Okay, okay!' And the lift closed. When he comes, she decided, we mustn't fail, we must come to the point. Why have I been so prim all this time? (Who am I keeping it for?) I'll ask him to stay and we'll have dinner . . . No, not here, how can I?

How could she, when all she had to cook on was a portable Camping Gaz with one burner? On this she fried her eggs and vegetables and sardines, she boiled spaghetti and then sauce, she brewed Greek coffee in a copper *briki*, she cooked her morning porridge, having found oats here at last, imported from Holland and very dear, in a grocer's near the flower market. What a luxury, after so long, to stir the thickening mass of oats until it plopped and then add honey in a trickle like a brass wire and eat it out of the saucepan! She always ate at home. Even in Sydney she was too shy ever to eat out alone; here women just didn't. In the covered market she bought her quarter-kilo of leeks here; her quarter-kilo of spilt sardines rusty with blood there; here an eighth of a kilo of olives, there a half-litre of dry red – '*brousko*', she insisted – Cretan wine. Shopkeepers exchanged resigned smiles when they saw her coming. On the way home, she stared in the steamy windows of the restaurants along Odos Egnatias at the crusted golden beans in earthenware, at roast meats wrapped in their film of fat . . .

I'll ask him out to a restaurant, she decided. I'll pay. Aleko can choose where. And then – what?

Her life had never seemed so empty to her as it did now that Aleko was the centre of it. She went on the bus to a cinema sometimes. She shopped and window-shopped. The streets were windy and stank of diesel fumes. She read in the warmth of the two libraries, the British Council one on the sea front and the United States Information Service one on Aristotelous Square, which was where Aleko had seen her notice offering lessons. (But he never happened to come in again while she was in there.) She borrowed books to take home, and returned them mostly unread: she was too cold, too restless, to be bothered.

On grey days her room could have been a cube of air cut inside an iceberg.

Once or twice a week she did her washing in the sink and pegged it out on a rope along the balcony, or up on the *taratsa*, the flat roof, with everyone else's, strung among dusty chimney pots and aerials; or even in the kitchen when it rained, and then her weak yellow bulb was screened by layers of washing that shed drips and shadows. She spread old newspapers – the *Times*, the airmail *Guardian*, bought for reading aloud with Aleko – over the powdery cement mosaic of her kitchen floor. She had a dream the morning of one washing day. She was hanging out a wet sheet in the wind when it became a sail, and a woman – who? – on a shore somewhere was leaning forward to tell her reproachfully, 'Life is so *ephemeral*.' The word itself was like a puff of air: *ephemeral*.

It stayed with her. She even looked it up in Greek: *efimero*, the same. Life was *efimero*. For days she was filled with a sense of urgency, of waste time. She was as housebound as an old widow, and she was all of twenty-eight.

She made herself go out for long walks. She sat on benches in the parks and ate the roast chestnuts or the corncobs that she bought on street corners, or a *souvlaki* in a paper bag. Men pestered her, gypsy women begged, gypsy boys smeared shoe polish on her suede boots and sneered in her protesting face. '*Raus!*' they called after her: all blond people were Germans.

One gypsy woman in particular, nursing a little red baby, worried Kay so much that she told Aleko about her: a gaunt woman whining out of a greasy scarf that let only her long brown teeth and nose show. Kay gave her ten drachmas. Aleko whistled at that. 'She'll remember *your* face,' he said. He believed the gypsy women took turns to hold the baby. But it really was a sick baby, it was yellow, with a crusted rash. Then there was the beggar woman at the Post Office counters, roaring with her hand stretched out at you, a tongueless and toothless giantess like a dead tree. She never failed to corner Kay. And sure enough, that gypsy with the sick baby ran into Kay all over the place as she photographed ruins – 'One earthquack do that,' Aleko explained – and huts and churches, and sculpted faces in the crowd. 'Tou*rist*?' furtive young men whispered behind her. 'Spik English, miss? Tou*rist*?'

No, she thought, never answering them though: I *live* in Thessaloniki. I live in Greece now.

The neighbours greeted her curtly when they met in the building. They shrieked at her when she swilled water on her balcony to wash the dust off and it piddled down the spout in a murky arc on to the footpath: though they all washed their balconies. They exchanged dark looks when they caught her seeing Aleko off at the lift. He was five years younger than she was, and looked younger still: their eyes said that this beautiful young man had undersold himself, because doubtless she was supporting him. How ludicrous she was, this lovesick broomstick, this *Anglida* of his! Kay took to not wearing her glasses, to make herself more worthy of Aleko. She knew her way in the blurred streets by now, and at home she could see everything except glasses and bottles, whose contents seemed to hang in mid-air in some disturbance of the light. During lessons – at the card table under her dim kitchen bulb – she sometimes had to bend in front of Aleko until her nose was on the page. She blushed. Could he see through her? If so, she thought, all he saw would be a burning scarlet flood of light . . .

On the morning of Saint Katerina's day Kay washed her hair, something she did less often now, it took so long to dry. She had what they called here a telephone shower, hand-held (but no bath or shower recess, so that it flooded the floor) and shivered in its lukewarm trickle every day. In September when she first came, she could squat on the *taratsa* and her hair ran like hot toffee over her bare knees, drying in minutes. Even on fine days now the sun had no warmth. That morning she dried her hair kneeling in front of the red bars of the radiator and pulling her fingers through the knots. With hours to fill in, on impulse she caught a throbbing blue bus to the city, to a tourist shop she knew, where she bought coloured candles and four hand-woven woollen *tagaria*, to use not as shoulder bags but as cushions. They made beautiful cushions with her summer clothes crammed in them, scattered on her bed – which was not ostentatiously her *bed*, since it was a rubber mat on the waxed planks of the bedroom floor with a *flokati* rug of tufted greasy wool over it instead of blankets. It wouldn't look too obvious, if they had their party there. *We hev little party*: that was sweet of him. She had coffee, sugar, brandy. The brandy was getting low, but a new bottle now would cut into the restaurant money. She stared in the mirror and spread over her velvet shoulders the polished stripes of her long hair. Would the sun never set? She lit the candles, switched on the radiator. Again and again, her heart jumping, she held her watch to her ear.

When at last the bell rang, she counted to ten first, before she opened the door. There stood Aleko, holding a large white box, red ribbons curled all over it. And beside him, a plump Greek girl. Gypsy-eyed, richly dark.

'Kay, hullo!' he shouted. '*Chronia polla!* Many heppy years!' He passed her the box, which automatically she took, her eyes fixed on his in her consternation. The girl, stepping forward, grabbed Kay's free hand in her warm brown one and shook it. '*Chronia polla,*' she said, 'Nitsa.'

'Nitsa?'

'. . . Yes. This is Nitsa,' Aleko said, his voice choked with self-consciousness and pride. 'Nitsa, this is my English teacher. This is Kay.'

They smiled, and Nitsa fluffed her tails of black hair loose with her hand. The corridor light clicked. They were in darkness. 'Well, come *in*.' Kay held the door open. 'Please, Nitsa, Aleko. Come in and sit down.' Who was it? Was she supposed to know? One of his sisters? She shut the door and with an embarrassed laugh led them to the *flokati* in her flickering room. They sat side by side on it, their backs to the wall, stretching their legs out to the red bars. Kay hovered in the doorway. 'May I open it?' She peeped, and did: in the box were six cream sponge cakes of the kind called *pastes*, thickly piped with cream and sanded with roast nuts. 'Oh look, *pastes*!' she managed – she who loathed cream.

'You like it?'

'*Love* it, thank you. Both. They look delicious.'

'Is o*kay*, Kay.'

'You hev a goot view,' offered the girl, Nitsa. The lamps had come on in the street, dripping and swaying at the water's edge. The *volta* was beginning, shadows were shuffling past. The whole sea was a dying fire. Beyond it the dark mountain stood; white lights glittered on it like sparks astray in winds.

'Mount Olympus,' Kay said reverently.

'Yes, you know Olimbos? He hev a lot of snow nown.'

'Now,' smiled Kay.

'Yes, nown snow. Is winter nown.'

Aleko rewarded Nitsa with a dazed smile and took her hand.

'These beautiful *pastes*. Let's have them now.' Kay held up the box and nodded to Nitsa. 'Nown?'

'No, no, Kay! Is all for you this one!'

'Aleko, I'd *die*. You have to help me. Well, excuse me, won't you?' They would . They smiled ecstatically.

In the kitchen she was frantic to remember. Aleko had mentioned sisters, hadn't he? Two sisters? Well, then! But no, one's name was Maria and the other one's? – Toula. Nitsa must be a cousin. Young men were expected to escort their cousins too. Her hands quivering, Kay lit the Camping Gaz and stirred coffee and water and sugar in the *briki*. She found plates and forks for the *pastes*. Pouring two glasses of her dark brandy, she drank one down, rinsed and refilled the glass. The coffee frothed. She tipped it into the cups – at least she had three *cups*. Please, Agia Aikaterini, Katerina, Katy, let Nitsa be a cousin, she thought. They were very quiet in there on the *flokati*.

Nitsa's hair was a shawl over Aleko, until they saw her and sat bolt upright. And Nitsa was not a cousin.

'*Stin ygeia sou*, Kay,' they chanted, tossing down their brandies. She served them a *pasta* each and, putting the tray of coffees on the floorboards near them, sat on a *tagari* cushion to munch her way through hers. They jabbed and licked and gulped. Once Aleko bent and stole a chunk off Nitsa's fork. 'Ach!' she squealed, delighted, and slapped his thigh. His teeth when he grinned were lathered with the cream. Kay smiled maternally.

'Aren't they de*lic*ious!' She rinsed her mouth with coffee. 'Where did you get them?'

'From very goot shop. Terkenli, you know, Kay,' he boasted. 'Is near to the American library.'

'They must have cost a fortune. You shouldn't have.'

'You hev to eat!' He sucked his coffee. 'Look at you, all bones, is no goot for your healthy. Not *you*, you too fet.' He poked Nitsa's waist. '*Patata eisai esi*. One big fet patato.'

'*Niata threfo*,' Nitsa said loftily. Kay raised her brows.

'She hev to feed her youngness, she say. Young pipple need to eat *too much*.'

'*Kala lei*,' agreed Kay. Her tone was dry; not that they noticed.

'*Ya!*' Nitsa grinned at her and gave Aleko a triumphant shove that sent him sprawling. They giggled. How old was Nitsa? Kay could just make out their faces on the coppery wall, half lit among shadows and reflected in the glass door now that the sky was dark. Perhaps sixteen; eighteen at the most. She licked her white fork.

'Well, I'm still hungry.' She made her voice light. 'I'm going to bring the other *pastes* now.'

'No, no,' said Aleko feebly. She took their plates anyway and dished out the other three *pastes* in the kitchen. This time she remembered water, pouring them two glasses that turned the gold of beer when she brought them in.

'And now more coffee,' she said.

'No, no. No, really, Kay.'

'You always have two or three coffees!'

'Yes, but no, Kay, sorry. We carn stay nown.'

They couldn't stay. So that was that.

'I hev auntie in Melvourni,' mumbled Nitsa with her mouth full. 'You come from Melvourni?'

'No, Sydney.'

'Ach, Sydnayee.'

'Is nice place, Sydnayee, Kay?'

'Yes. It's like here in some ways. A city on the sea – '

'Like here? Is so cold?'

'Well, no – it's summer there now, of course.'

'*Po po*! Summer there nown!' Nitsa giggled with a great shudder. Aleko tugged the *flokati* up around her shoulders.

'You look like Eskimo,' he said happily, combing her back with dark fingers. 'One big fet Eskimo bear.'

Kay shut her eyes to remember Sydney and in what ways it was like here. But Sydney was a set of faded transparencies. What her parents wanted was their old

Kay back. As for those of her old friends who were still there, what did she have to say to them? As much as she had to say to these two. *I zoï*, she thought she might say, as one who leans earnestly forward across widening water: *I zoï eina toso efimeri* –

'We hev to visit another Katerinas, many Katerinas tonight,' Nitsa was explaining. Kay nodded.

'You lookink too sed, Kay.' He bent to help Nitsa up, brushing her crumbs off. 'I think so you hev nostalgear nown.'

'Oh, a little bit. No, not really. I'm happy.' She scrambled up. 'It's been a lovely party, thank you both.'

'Well, I see you next lesson. Hey, silly me!' He glowed, all eagerness. 'I forgot to say you. Din I say I find you one new student? Well: Nitsa want to learn with me English!'

'. . . Oh. Yes, Nitsa? Oh, good.'

'We learnink together, okay? Is more funny.'

'Fun. Yes, I see.' Kay laughed indignantly, and he mistook her.

'We come together and both of us payink you sixty *drachmes*,' he said quickly. 'One hundred twenty. Okay – Kay?'

'Okay. That will be fun.' She smiled back at them. When they come next time, she thought, I can always say that my mother's sick and I have to go home. I don't have to stay in Thessaloniki or in Greece if I don't want to. Can I stay here now? How the neighbours would laugh if they knew! They laughed anyway.

She got rid of Aleko and Nitsa (who were more than anxious to be gone) and rinsed the dishes, leaving them to dry on the marble, the real marble, of the draining board. In her room she locked the balcony shutters and straightened the still-warm *flokati*, which smelled of Arpège. To think I hoped he could love *me*, she thought: it never even crossed his mind. (Though it must have crossed Nitsa's, clever little Nitsa's.) It seemed to Kay now that nothing more would ever happen to her; her life would never be any fuller than it was at this moment, in this lonely city or another.

Mewings, scratchings at the front door: wearily she let the cat in. It was greedy and luxurious, not lovable at all. It sniffed, peering round. She gave it its milk cold. It wet its nose, gazed up with a mew, backed away. When it was sure the milk wouldn't warm itself, it stalked to her cushion and curled up with its back to her. The lizard hadn't come out. Nitsa must have alarmed it: it knew Aleko. Maybe it was going torpid and would freeze stiff in this cold, not coming alive till spring. So might she, here. A moth, quivering loudly at her ear, stumbled away among the candle flames. Fire would eat the moth, or the cat would, or the lizard. *Efimero, efimero!* As for her, she had nothing to eat in the flat, not even a drop of *brousko* wine. She had to keep her strength up. How had Nitsa put it? *Niata threfo. Niata*, youth: well, hardly . . .

Kay took out her tin of oats and ran her fingers through the flakes. She could always have porridge for dinner, porridge with bright honey. But wasn't there something stringy in the oats? She stared. Webs of them clung to her fingers. Yes, the oats were strung on webs, like corks on a fishing net. She could have wailed aloud. Weevils had got into the oats!

No, it was too much. Biting her lips, she lit the Camping Gaz and put the tin of oats on the flame. Let them bake in it like silkworms in their cocoons: why should she throw her Dutch oats out? As she watched, though, a little horrified, a white grub broke the surface of the flakes and reared, waved itself at full length, hopped and hurled itself first on to the red-hot rim, then on to the floor. She knelt and peered. Where was it on the cement mosaic? What a heroic escape! She had read, in an American magazine at the library, about a man tied with ropes and thrown on to an anthill in a pit rearing like that: covered in red skeins of ants he reared to his feet, to his full height, in the agony of death. The grub had done that. But it was still alive, wasn't it? It had to be!

She turned the Camping Gaz off – there might be others still alive – and jammed on her glasses. In the thick yellow light she crouched down, slanting to throw her shadow aside, and felt with her fingertips every chip and speckle of the floor where the grub had fallen. But she found only dust.

Against her shoulder the Burmese cat came pushing its warm head, purring. Then it hunched, stared, danced around the table legs and, before Kay could move, patted something and licked it up. *'Pussy!'* she groaned. It closed blissful eyes, in its mincing delicacy like a furred brown spider. Pinching its scruff in her powdery fingers, she dropped it outside in the dark of the corridor and slammed the door. The flat reeked of singed oats.

'You blight on the earth,' she told her reflection in the pane. 'The futility of you!' Her face flashed, goggling back. She pulled off her glasses to wipe her eyes. And then: 'Crying over a dead grub! What would the neighbours think of the mad *Anglida* if they saw you now? Wouldn't they be right, too?' Because she could see the ludicrous side of it all, but only as if at a great distance . . . Saint Kay's day! Life is so *efimeri*! Oh dear, oh dear. I *will* go out, she thought suddenly, I'll go out for dinner anyway. At one of those restaurants with steamy panes in Odos Egnatias (but I'll take a book with me). I'll have Cretan *brousko* wine, blood-red in the copper measuring beaker, and crusty beans or meat out of an earthenware baking dish . . . She would go somewhere warm with fuzzy gold lights and an uproarious crowd, where you stayed as long as you wanted: out there in the real Thessaloniki. And then? Then – come back here?

Besides, she wasn't hungry any more, not after the *pastes*, not after the oats.

In the cave of her bedroom she lay back with her hair spread out on the hot tufts of the *flokati*. The radiator hummed its one note. Veils of the candlelight began their frilling and soft unravelling on the whitewash. After a while the lizard came out and sunned himself. After a while, she could have been anywhere in the world. Saint Kay's day was as good as over. One month to Christmas

Day, she thought: and knew that, wherever in the world she was at Christmas, she would be there among strangers. The shadows of small flames quivered over her. She was sleepy now. She lay, a log in a sinking fire.

AT THE AIRPORT

Her son clatters into the airport building, impatient to go. She gloats over him, his wheaten hair, his eyes the same colour of dark honey that his father's are, his sturdy long body and legs. He is eight and she will not see him again for three months. Again he is going with his father, who used to be her husband, to spend the winter, the Greek summer, in his grandparents' village. He will write to her.

Dear Mum haw ar you good you shod come one day it is
relly fun we have watafites and jamp off the hen house.
Grand Dad is all ways snoring i can not go to sleep! Zzzz
i wish we cod stay here. love from me and Dad and Grand
Mum and Grand Dad and the rest off the famaly X X X X
X X X X X X   PAUL

He will send photographs of himself with his grandparents, who were fond of their foreign daughter-in-law. She will see him grinning into the sun in villages and on beaches that she will never go to again. As time passes they are becoming like the house she keeps dreaming of, which has never existed, she is sure, yet which she recognizes when she goes there.

She will miss him. He will not really miss her. They no longer live together and haven't for four years. He stays at her flat on weekends and school holidays. For all this, her ex-husband blames her. Her mother, who is dead, blamed her. Her son, more than anyone else, blames her.

*

Her ex-husband, flustered and tired, waits in line to check in his luggage. The girl he lives with now fills in his

immigration cards for him. To give the couple time
alone, her son and she go to the cafeteria. On the way
they buy a doll for a new baby cousin in Greece whose
godfather her son is going to be. She herself will never see
this baby girl. Photographs will show him taking a wet
and oily naked baby from the bearded priest, just as six
years ago he was taken, splashing and furious. She buys a
coffee, and a trifle for him. She asks for a taste. He gives
her spoon for spoon of it, sandy, soaked with wine.

'I thought you liked trifle?' She is disappointed.

'Oh yes, I do.'

'But you've given me half?'

'Well, you like it too. Don't you?'

His smile is sad. He is sorry for her, because he is going
and she is not.

*

They are stopping over in Bangkok. She remembers
her son at two on his father's shoulders at a rainy temple
in Bangkok, a flounced and gilded temple full of a statue
of Buddha. A cat lapped a puddle in which grey pigeons
and the gold robes of monks were reflected, fluttering.
He climbed down to stroke the crouched cat.

She remembers him that year on the shoulders of an
uncle emerging from the dark vault of a mulberry grove
into the noon heat. He munched, stained with juice. His
hands made crimson prints on his uncle's bald dome.
They washed each other at a tap in the yard. His white
hair trickled. Seeing her, he opened his arms and leaped
into hers. He was glossy, cold-skinned. '*Moura*,' he said.
Mulberries.

That year he was baptised in the font of the village
church. He was given his Greek name, his grandfather's:
Pavlo. And Greek nationality.

*

After drinks at the bar and hasty kisses and farewells
they are gone. She is left with Vanessa, who lives with
them now but has never gone with them, not yet. She

and Vanessa go back together to sit in the bar beside a window through which they can see all the plane. It is late taking off. She is sipping riesling and Vanessa vermouth. They are not alike in any way. Even the man each of them has loved in her time is not the same man. She looks in the pane at the sleek eyes and hair of this younger woman warmly nestled, looking out. No sadness is showing. She sees herself, looking no less calm. Their glances, meeting, jump away.

The plane taxies and turns. They stand to watch it hurl itself up. Then they take polite leave of each other.

She pays her parking fee at the gate and drives on to the freeway. Planes in the foggy air blink their lights and rise and sink. There is a dim full moon. It will shrink and fill again three times before his father brings him back. He must, he has made promises. No self-pity, she thinks, having worked hard to keep her composure, the outward sign of dignity, intact. It is her crust, her shell. Her carapace. Loss and the fear of loss assail her.

*

'Daddy wants us to go and live in Greece now,' she remembers him saying a while ago. 'But you can come too.'

'I couldn't go and live in Greece, Paulie.'

'You used to.'

'Ages ago. I don't belong there now.'

'Why not?'

'I just don't.'

'*I* do.'

'Yes, I know.'

'I'm Greek.'

'Half-Greek.'

'No. I'm Greek.'

'Well, I'm not.'

'You can speak Greek.'

'That's not enough.' She hugged him. 'You belong here too.'

'There's better, Mum.'

'Why?'

'Well, *there's* a family.'

*

In the next two months she is patient. She goes to her job in a coffee shop and then to classes. She hands in work on time. She sleeps late. She walks along the winter beaches. On the grey sand she finds mussel shells, feathers, dulled glass. She sees a yacht trail close in to shore. Its heavy sails move cloud-coloured, the late sun in them. Out past the shore water shadowed by this or that drift of wind, a red ship hangs in midair.

She remembers their summer beaches. She dwells on the time when he was four, only four, and they were in Greece for the last time together. She blew up his yellow floaties on his arms, took his hand and swam with him in tow far out into the deep water where a yacht was anchored. Puffing, they clung to a buoy rope that threw bubbles of water in a chain on the surface of the sea. Scared and proud, they waved to his father and the rest of the family, those dots on the sand, aunts and uncles and cousins. The yacht tilted creaking above them. On the sea, as if in thick glass, its mast wobbled among clouds. They glided back hand in hand. Used to waters where sharks might be, she had never dared swim out so far before. Here there were none. They passed, mother and son, above mauve skeins of jellyfish suspended where the water darkened, but not one touched them. Bubbles had clustered, she saw, on the fine silver hairs on his back, on his brown legs and arms and on hers.

She often dreams of this swim now. It was a month after it, back home in the early spring, that she left home. Her son was asleep. When he woke he thought Mummy was playing hidey. He laughed, looking in wardrobes. Then his father told him. 'Your Mummy's sick in hospital,' he said. Her son told her all this later. 'Well, what I should say?' his father shouted at her. 'You walk out, you want I say that?'

She found a flat in South Melbourne, two hours' drive

from their town, and a job in a hotel. 'I thought you'd be a good mother,' was what her mother said. 'You were at first.'

*

Her son's black kitten, black but for the circles of gold round his eyes, sits and nibbles one paw. He has been entrusted to her while her son is away. He is used to her now. He falls asleep on her lamb's fleece stretched on his back. When he wakes the bell at his throat will tell her so. At night she sits and studies. A cowled white lamp peers over her shoulder at the shadow of her hand writing. The kitten wakes – chink – and gazes. He eats crouching, his sharp little shoulders almost bald. She lets him out during the day, but is anxious. At night he must use the litter box. He prowls in it and flips the granules over the carpet obsessively. Nothing must happen to him while he is at her place. Growth, of course, must. He is becoming a stolid cat. Will her son still love him? Will her son come back?

On her balcony she listens to a slow sonata, a hollow clarinet, watching a sunset douse its cold flames in the bay. The bridge has its gold lights on. The moon, when it rises, is nearly full again. The moon she sees tonight shone a few hours ago over her son. Does he ever think of her? Remember me, she says. Miss me. I miss you.

The pot of basil they gave her for her balcony before they left is still there, but black and dry. Basil dies in winter. Her balcony faces the sea wind. The lane opposite is always full of dark rainwater. The sunset shows in it. Night fills it with lamps.

*

'It's breaking your mother's heart,' a neighbour reproved her when she first left. It was true, in a way. Her mother's little clockwork voice was always on the phone.

'I've talked to a lawyer,' it piped. 'Act fast, she says. The longer you delay the more weight it gives to the status quo.'

'Delay – what?'

'You have to *apply* for interim custody. You can't wait till the divorce.'

'Oh, Mum, no, I can't contest custody.'

'What do you mean? He's not going to hand you the child on a platter. He'll fight you for him.'

'He talked about that before I left. Even if I won he wouldn't let me get away with it. He'd kidnap him and go home. He would.'

'There are laws –'

'Constantly being broken. You know that.'

'Well, try, at least. What's got into you?'

'That'd turn him completely against me.'

'So *what?*'

'Mum, as things are, he lets me see Paul. And he lets *you* see Paul. He's sorry for us.'

'Why should anyone be sorry for you? You've brought it on yourself. Where did I go wrong? A real mother would go to hell and back to keep her child!'

*

She writes to Paul about his kitten and the football and the village. She knows it amazes him that she knows the village. He forgets that she went there before he was born and then twice with him when he was little. With an incredulous grin he looks at slides of her in the village with his family, when he comes to visit, as if she was there by some magic. She knows how he feels.

She takes out the old projector and looks at the slides again. She gets photographs from him in the mail and studies them. She gets a letter.

Dear Mum haw ar you i am very well evry day we go to the beche, evry after noon the weves have gron hiarh and hiarh and moore hiarh and hiarh. i went very deep on tuesday. how is my cat. there is a kitten here its names psipsina. i was bitten by a wosp on the neck twis i was pritending i was drackula. any way love from me and evry body X X X X X X X X X X PAUL

He used to ask her why. Why don't you love my Dad?
Why did you leave us? (Why didn't you wake me? Take
me?) Won't you ever come back? Why not? Will you
always be my mother?

He would understand one day, she used to answer: it
was a long story. She doesn't ever want to show him
wounds or admit to the rage and spite that caused them.
Nor, she thinks, does his father. They both cringe under
their son's accusing gaze. They have stopped accusing
each other, and now make what amends they can. They
trust each other to behave well. It was not always so.

What matters after all is that there came, in their anger
and terror and despair, a point of silence one night in
which she went to her sleeping child, kissed his cheek,
picked up her suitcase. Left. This is what counts. Might it
have been otherwise? Yes. No. Whatever happened
before it belongs to one life, which is over. What comes
after is another. In dreams, what is meshes with what was
and what might have been; as in dreams she goes to a
remembered house which does not exist. What might
have been cannot be.

Since Vanessa moved in, he has stopped asking
questions.

*

She brought him to stay at her new flat and took him to
the Zoo. Politely they gazed at the animals, especially the
sandy, sleepy lions. He rode on the train and on a white
pony. On the spiral slide he made her go up with him the
first time and clung to her as they spun down; then he
went up alone again and again while she waited to catch
him at the bottom. They had hamburgers and milk
shakes. Then he had to go to the toilet. The Men's, he
insisted. She promised to wait but after a while she called
out that she was just going to the Women's: wait, she
said. When she came out he was not there. She stood in
the smelly shade until a man looked in and told her there
was no little boy inside. She rushed over to the lions, then
to the slide, the ponies, the train, the toilets again. A

microphone blared. Reception! she thought and hurtled along crowded paths. There he was, red-faced. He turned his back.

'A lady brought him in. He said his Mummy went home!' the woman at Reception accused. 'Of course I said Mummies don't do that, but he was that positive! "Why ever would she?" I said and he said, "I don't know."'

'I was only in the toilet,' she explained.

'You were not!'

'I was. I called out.'

'You did *not*!'

'Darling, I *did*! You just didn't hear.'

'No, you never! You did not call out! Oh, why didn't you?'

She tried to hug him and wipe his eyes. Sobbing, he pushed her. But he walked beside her out into the sun.

'Remember our long swim?' she asked as they watched lions.

'In Greece?'

'Yes. Remember?'

'No,' he muttered.

*

One afternoon the cat doesn't come back in. She wanders, calling, along streets filled with cars and darkness. The lamps twitch on. The pairs of gold eyes that she stalks and chases all belong to strange cats. His cat must be lost. The wind tugs and hurls cold sea-spray. She blunders through puddles.

At home in the lamplight she can't concentrate on work. She can't finish her letter to her son. A child is wailing in the flat next door. Mama. Ma-ama. Every half hour she goes to the door and calls the cat.

Once as her son stepped out of her car after a visit with her, he saw his kitten playing on the road. He called, but the kitten lifted his tail and danced away. 'If I catch him I'll kill him!' Her son's face was dark red. 'He knows he's not allowed out! I'll kill him!'

'Oh, Paulie,' she said.

'I will. I mean it. I'll flush him down the toilet!'

'He'll come back,' she said.

He just looked at her.

Before she goes to bed she opens the door a last time and calls out. Suddenly the cat is there, flattened against the wall in the wind, thin and black as his shadow. He struts in and prowls, purring, and folds himself on the lamb's fleece.

*

After the divorce, when her ex-husband took her son home to Greece, her mother would not be consoled. Paul was gone, her only grandchild. He was as good as gone before that. But now his father would never bring him back.

'Mum, he will.'

'What makes you think so?'

'He just will.' Compassion, she thought. Respect for the tacit bargain: you keep him, but *here*. Even mercy, for the defeated opponent. 'His business, for one thing.'

'Why did you have to go and marry a Greek?'

'Oh, come on. You always liked him.'

'Can't you work something out?'

'No.'

'I can't get over it. How could you do it?'

'I had to.'

'It wasn't that bad.'

'It *was*. I was spending days staring at one corner in one room. The sun never came in. Everything was grey. Shadows moved, that was all. Nothing mattered, not even the child, and he was so persistent. When footsteps came near me, I banged my head on the window frame until it bled or they went away.'

'You should have seen a doctor.'

'A doctor! When my *life* – '

'A doctor, yes. Depression can be treated, you know.'

'I've come alive since I left.'

' "I, I, I." When you realise how selfish you've been

all along, and how *weak*, when you finally think of the *child* – '

'It's best for him not to be fought over.'

'You *hope*. Oh, the easy way out, as per usual. You're a callous and self-centred woman. I'm ashamed you're my daughter.'

*

'You make better chips than Vanessa,' her son told her on a visit a few months ago.

'That's good. Who's Vanessa?'

'A lady. She lives at our place. She's got this dog. Its name's Roly. Guess why.'

'Short for Roland?'

'No. Because it's always rolling! Mum, if my Dad marries Vanessa, will Roly be in my family?'

'I suppose. Vanessa. She's not Greek, is she?'

'No. She comes from Sydney.'

'Has she been to Greece, do you know?'

'Yes. She loves it. She'd like to live there, she says. Could she take Roly?'

'I don't know. Maybe. Is he friendly?'

'Oh, yes. You make the best chips I've ever aten.'

'Eaten.'

'Eaten.'

*

They did come back from Greece that first time, and the next. Her son loved her mother just the same after the divorce, and she spoiled him. Now, two years since her death, he often mentions Granma, his voice hushed and sorrowful. He remembers her best cooking dinners when they visited, ladling gravy, hovering over a sizzled chicken. He knows he will die one day. He buries dead birds and crickets, and saves moths from his cat.

One morning in September she has a good dream. She is at the house she is always dreaming of. It has a deep verandah of sagging boards that looks on to muddy grass and bare trees. A window burns with light. As the sun sets she strolls in and opens a door of gold wood that she has never opened in any previous dream. She knows the moment before she looks that her son will be in there. He is asleep, his cat at his feet. He wakes and looks up, smiling.

She lies awake breathless with joy in her rented bed. She wishes she could tell her mother this dream. Some time, she hopes, her mother will be behind a door, in one of the bright rooms in this house.

*

Dear Mum haw ar you we ar coming back 15 september. its at 4 oclock in the morning. pleas meet us at the air port. i wont you to. X X X X X X X X X X   PAUL

*

She rings the number Vanessa has given her, but is told that Vanessa is up in Sydney because her mother is sick. So Vanessa won't be at the airport. On the night she wakes to the alarm with a sour headache at three, crams the cat into his basket and drives through the dark under all the faint lamps of the city. The airport building, full of light, is crowded already. Voices boom, echoing. The plane has landed. After an hour passengers start bursting through the door with luggage trolleys. Her eyes are crusted, dazed. They will keep watering. Her ex-husband and her son push through last of all. Her ex-husband looks smaller, gaunt and grey. But her son! So big, so brown! She is full of exclamations and this delights him. He thinks she is crying, though she says no. They all talk at once and wish aloud for coffee, but there is nowhere open, so they go out to the car-park. She has forgotten where she left her car. In the cold wind and half-light they all wander over the painted asphalt, look-ing. Her son sees it first. He wraps himself in his sullen cat. The sun comes up, a gong on the rim of the sky.

'Glad you're back?' She hugs Paulie.

'Yes, if you are.'

'I am. I'm very glad.' To her ex-husband she says in

Greek, 'There are times when –' She can't speak. 'Life –'
she tries again.

'Oh, life. Life. Well, yes.' He smiles wanly.

The trees toss and swill the gold light. Their eyes
glitter with it.

ISMINI

Behind its hooded verandah the house was deep in evening shadow. Ismini unlocked the front door, trudged through the green gloom to the kitchen and dumped her schoolbag on the plastic table cloth among long slabs of late sun. A fly nodded, stroking its hinged legs.

With a wince she unwrapped the two slimy speckled translucent squids and rinsed them under the tap. Their beaks and torn eyes had to be prised out, then the fretted glassy backbones, the inksacs. She cut up the ornate tentacles and the sheaths of their bodies. She made a salad glowing green and red, put it with the *retsina* and the blubbery squid in the refrigerator, poured a glass of milk and sat down to her homework.

One morning on a hot wooden jetty her father had hauled a squid out of the flashing sea. Dripping, its bright mantle fading, it had shuddered and wheezed at her feet, blind in the white sun, as it died.

Oh, what is it, Baba?

Kalamari.

Mummy, Baba's caught a kamalari!

Oh yes, look. A squid.

In English it was a different creature.

*

'Write a pen-portrait of a person you know well. The subject's appearance, attitudes, way of life, character, should be covered. 250-500 words.'

She scribbled notes. My Grk grandmother. Yiayia Sophia. Will Mrs Brown object if the subject is dead? She won't know. Red eggs for Easter, the lamb on the iron spit, the awful offal soup. The brain broiled in the charred skull. Mother cat, kittens buried alive. Bad luck to kill a cat. Perpetual mourning.

A hard marker, Mrs Brown had said that Ismini was clever and should have no trouble getting a studentship to Teachers' College, if that was what she wanted. Mrs Brown had said after class that she might need Ismini to baby-sit on Saturday if her live-in girl was still ill. Oh yes, I'd love to, Mrs Brown.

The deep sun was making Ismini's face burn like a brass gong in the window pane, like the mask of Agamemnon, long-eyed, long-lipped. Her breasts lay round and heavy under her uniform. She fingered her warm hair.

Doan be hard on your Yiayia, Ismini *mou*. She give up everythink to come out here, look after us.

We didn't need her, Baba, did we?

We need her, you know that. She been like a mother to you.

She's always picking on me.

She just frighten. She tell your Theia she see your mother in you.

Oh does she? Good!

Baba once said Ismini could cook squid better than Mummy could, even better than Yiayia. These squids were fresh ones from the market especially for his birthday. Out of her pocket money she had bought real Greek *feta* cheese and the *retsina* and a carton of the Greek cigarettes he loved, Assos Filtro, supplied by Poppy's sister, an air hostess. In Greece, Baba said, they didn't celebrate birthdays. Mummy loved birthdays. If Mummy had been Greek and not Australian, who knew if she would have left home like that? Theia Frosso said no Greek woman would. Today there was no letter, no birthday card, in the box. Yet they had been one flesh.

She had run into Mummy the other day by chance in the Mall. She had stopped to chat, her own mother, grinning and tapping her foot on the hot tramlines, lighting a quick cigarette and blowing out smoke. She was really sorry to have to rush off like this.

I saw Mummy in town today, Baba.

Doan talk to me about that bitch.

'Ismini?' Theia Frosso was shrilling from outside. Ismini sighed. Theia Frosso, not her real aunt but Baba's second cousin, lived next door and felt responsible. The doors slammed. She strutted in, kissed Ismini and sank on to her usual chair.

'Ach! All alone, you poor gel, why you doan come an watch television with the kids, eh?'

'I haven't even started my homework, Theia.'

Ismini poured her the daily, the ritual dose of sweet vermouth; caught a coil of her orange-peel preserve glowing and porous in the jar of heavy syrup and set it still in the spoon on a glass dish; poured iced water; mixed coffee for two in the red *briki*. It frothed and sputtered in the gas flame. She bit her lip.

'It boil out? Is nothing. *Yeia mas*.' Theia Frosso ate and drank and licked her lips. 'I tell you, your Baba, he a very lucky, he hev a daughter like you look after him. A good little Greek housewive.'

'I'm not really Greek.'

'What you tokkink about? You Greek.'

Theia Frosso lit a cigarette and turned the coffee cups upside-down to read the future in the grounds. Yet Theia Frosso was *moderna*: she encased her flab in pantsuits, she dyed her hair red, she smoked cigarettes.

The telephone rang.

'Hullo?'

Theia Frosso was intent.

'Ismini? Hullo, love, it's me. Look, somethink's come up, I be home late. Sorry, eh? You doan mind, do you, love?'

'Well, how late will you be?'

'Dunno for sure. Doan wait up.'

'You won't be home for dinner?'

'Doan worry, I grab a *souvlaki*.'

'Baba, I got *kalamaria*!'

'Tomorrow. We hev them tomorrow. Sorry, love, I

gotta go, I double-parked. Make sure you lock up, all right?'

'All right. *Yeia sou.*'

'*Yeia.*'

She slammed the phone down. Happy birthday, Baba.

'He hev gel fren.' Theia Frosso giggled, inspecting the brown ripples in Ismini's cup. 'You hev to expect. A taxi–driver metink lotsa people. He still a quite yunk men, you know thet.'

'So what if he has?'

'He never tell you, *kale*, he be shame.'

'Why should he be?'

'Mama? Eh, Mama?' Theia Frosso's scrawny youngest was shrilling out over the grey fence. She rose sighing, her duty done at least, stubbed out her cigarette, planted more rubber kisses.

'Without me they carn do nothink. Sorry, I betta go. You come an hev dinner, eh? Why you wanna stay here all alone? No good for you.'

'Too much to do, Theia.'

Ismini rinsed the dishes. The sun had left the window in a bronze haze. She switched the sallow bulb on and sat down under it to write.

MY GREEK GRANDMOTHER

My Greek grandmother, Yiayia Sophia, was swathed in her widow's mourning clothes and headscarf until she died. Her mouth was folded over her toothless gums, her skin yellow and creased, her grey hair worn in two long pigtails even in bed. A wick floating in oil on water kept a flame sputtering all night in front of the ikon in her room.

She knew all the prayers. All through Lent she fasted until she could hardly stand, her candle shaking, outside the church at the Easter midnight service. There were fireworks hanging and flaring, and we all cracked our red eggs and ate them and nursed our candle flames all the way home for luck. Then we had to eat her magieritsa.

I remember her hoarding our hens' eggs for days beforehand and hard-boiling them on Holy Thursday in red dye. We

*polished them, still warm, with cloths dipped in oil. She
baked plaited* tsoureki *loaves. She made the* magieritsa, *the
traditional soup of lamb offal, flushing out the lungs and
entrails with the garden hose, screeching at the avid hens,
stirring it all in the pot with onions and herbs like a witch at
her cauldron.*

*The lamb itself my father had skinned and impaled on an
iron rod. Its red eye-sockets, its grinning teeth with the spit
thrust out like an iron tongue. All Easter Sunday morning it
was twisted and basted over the trench of coals, speckled with
charred herbs, while it turned dark brown and neighbours and
relatives danced to the record player on the back lawn. When
they split the skull for my grandmother, she offered me a
forkful of the brains.*

'Eat it, silly,' she cackled. 'God gave it to us.'

'Ugh, no! I don't want it.'

She shrugged, mumbling the grey jelly.

*Our cat had kittens once. A lovely pure black cat, a
witch-cat, she lay purring, slit-eyed, as they butted and
squeaked at her pink teats. Our cat was necessary, as the hens
attracted mice. Kittens weren't. One day the cat was crying
and clawing at a damp patch of ground under the tomatoes. I
dug up the corpses, their fur and tiny mouths and moonstone
eyes all clogged with earth. I accused Yiayia.*

'Don't be silly,' was all she said.

*She is dead and buried herself now, in foreign earth. I saw
her dying, her old mouth agape fighting for breath; and dead
in her coffin at last, a yellow mask and folded lizard-claws.
She was always too old to love me. I'm too old to hate her any
more.*   *(430 words)*

At the funeral Baba had sobbed on Theia Fosso's
shoulder. Mummy hadn't been there. Ismini shuddered.
In her old sepia wedding picture nailed up beside the
ikon, Yiayia had Ismini's face: everyone said so. Ismini
had wanted to burn all the photos, but Baba made her put
them back up in the hollow room. There was one of
Mummy in Greece, on a plump donkey with her legs
sticking stiffly out; Baba was there, and Yiayia, swathed

even then, and a crowd of solemn children with shaved heads. Mummy looked happy.

The phone rang. Ismini's lip curled. So he was sorry, was he? Well, better late than never.

'Yes.'

'Hullo? That's you, Ismini, is it? Oh good.'

'Oh! Mrs Brown!'

When she had just finished the essay!

'I was hoping you'll still be free to baby-sit for us this Saturday. Have I left it too late?'

'Oh yes, I'd love to!'

'Oh good. The thing is, though, we'll be very late home. Will your parents let you stay the night?'

The wood-fire whispering, Ismini thought, flaring over the crammed bookshelves and the sofa bed in the bow window.

'Oh, yes!'

If Baba says no this time, then I'll leave home.

'You're sure? Oh good. I'll pick you up at seven on Saturday, then. Can you hear the bub bawling his head off? I'd better go. 'Bye, Ismini.'

The first time she stood for ten minutes on their front verandah, too nervous to knock. When she asked Mrs Brown what to do if the baby cried, the eight-year-old scoffed, but the two-year-old patted her knee: I'll help you, Minnie, he said. He always stops for me.

They sat round the fire while she read them Little Golden Books; calling her Minnie Mouse, exploding with giggles, chanting Meany, Meany, when she said lights out at nine.

I'm eight. I don't have to go to sleep yet.

You do so. Mummy said. He does so have to, Minnie.

Shut up you.

It was a funny name though, a fancy classical name, a whim of her pompous old godfather's, when she should have been called Sophia after Yiayia. His wife had lapped Ismini in rosy withering flesh, pressing lips soft as a cocoon on her wincing cheeks. Once her parents split up, her godparents stopped visiting. Only her name was left of them.

If Baba said no, she couldn't stay the night, then she'd ring Mummy. No, don't be silly. The last time, a man had picked up the phone. Lyn, it's for you, he'd called.

Mummy, it's me. Can you come over just for a while? Baba's gone out. Can you, please?

Darling, no, sweet, you know I can't, I have to get up at five to go to work —

I want to talk to you!

Well go ahead, sweet, what's the matter?

Baba says I can't go to Poppy's birthday party.

Oh, lovey, I'm sorry. What a shame.

I'm sixteen! I'm not a child! The whole form's going. He won't let me go anywhere. Please, will you just ring and talk to him?

He wouldn't listen to me. You know that. God, I'm the last person —

I'm sorry. You're otherwise engaged, aren't you?

Ah, Ismini —

She'd cut Mummy off. Mummy hadn't tried to ring back. Baba had been right all along, of course: forget about your Mummy, Ismini *mou*, she doan want you. Sixteen, Ismini said aloud, is old enough to leave home legally. She wondered if Poppy would like to share a flat.

It was getting late. She trailed down the dark passage to her father's room. Its velvet curtains were the same, like sleek brown fur, and the painted-over fireplace in the wall, and in the wardrobe doors those long hazed mirrors that she and Mummy had always polished together. She had dressed up and posed in the dim mirrors. Baba slept alone now. When nightmares had woken her he had come and carried her in to sleep between their big warm bodies.

Mummy's old forgotten red nightdress lay hidden under sheets in the bottom drawer. Ismini undressed to slip it on: it fitted now. She stroked Red Ruby on her lips and cheeks, and rimmed her long eyes with kohl. She brushed out her hair. In the blurred gold of the mirror a dusty ghost looked back.

Once, black and faceless against a half-light from the passage, Mummy had stooped over her, dragged down her pants and crammed a suppository like an iron spit up her bottom. She had had to rush out to the toilet, her bowels surging and snorting. Poppy said sex hurt like that. Poppy was raped.

Room by room Ismini snapped on the lights and checked that all the doors and windows were locked. Yiayia's room of dead faces, the kitchen, laundry, bathroom, the musty sitting room, and her own room last.

She had been lying awake, trying to make sense of their jumbled shouts in the kitchen, when Mummy had come bursting in, sobbing and shuddering, and slammed the door. They clung together in the dark until at last Baba's yells and crashes petered out, daring only to whisper.

I'm leaving. This time I'm leaving.

What's happened?

He's insane. He's capable of anything. God, I hate that man!

But what about me?

I'll have to go into hiding. I'll find somewhere to live where he won't find me. Ring you at school.

I'm coming with you!

No, sweet, you can't. He won't let you go. He'd stop at nothing if I took you. He said so.

Mummy, don't go. Don't, please.

In the chill of daybreak they found him asleep with his head in his bloodstained arms on the kitchen table glittering with smashed glass. Mummy crept past with her suitcase. Ismini draped his jacket over his wet shoulders, switched off the light, and crawled back into bed.

Now Mummy got up before daybreak and stood waiting among furled glittering lamps and skeletons of trees for the first golden tram to trundle up wrapped in fog like a caterpillar in a cocoon.

If I fail HSC, Ismini had remarked the other day, you can get me a job at the hotel with you.

Oh, you'll pass. Still want to be a teacher?

I don't know what I want.

In the kitchen Ismini lit the stump of her Easter candle and switched off the light to watch the little flame flap and tower. She thought of opening the *retsina*. No. Well, why not? She prised the cap off and filled a glass with the acrid wine. Happy birthday, Baba. She drank it in gulps, and ate all the salad, since it wouldn't keep, dipping chunks of bread in the juice, sucking the olive pits. Lovely ripe plums for later.

By candlelight her arms shone, and her breasts too, only half hidden in crimson silk.

You're so beautiful, he would say, sitting opposite, and she would smile mockingly over the rim of her glass at this dark tall grave man, a man who had lived, who had known sorrow. His name? What did it matter? He would bend to heap hot kisses on her hands.

Ah! But you're too innocent, my darling.

I'm so tired of innocence. Slowly, significantly.

God! Don't tempt me! And overcome by a wave of passion, crushing her fiercely in his arms, he would carry her limp and golden to her bed.

Ismini took a long swig and held her glass against the swelling candleflame. Light swung rocking all over her, the kitchen walls, the window panes. The luminous crimson plums sat glowing there. She bit one through its skin and its juice spurted.

Darling, she murmured out loud across the table. Oh, my darling.

DARLING ODILE

On the way from Sydney to Tahiti I stood for hours
every day at the ship's rail and gazed into the wake:
Tahiti, the Island of Love. Whales, under their mirroring
roof of waves, the tossed balloon of the green sun, must
be shrilling, wallowing, coupling. I tried to see dolphins
and flying fish. At night, hot in a daze of red Algerian
wine, I watched the mast point creaking to this star and
that, while under the lifeboats red cigarettes glowed,
faded, glowed like far lighthouses. A ukulele twanged
and voices sang.

I had brought a sleeping bag but Hamid, the Madagas-
can cabin 'boy' – Hamid was fifty if a day – said not to
think of sleeping on Tahitian beaches, whatever I might
be used to back home. No, he said, let me find somewhere safe for you, *chérie*.

Before lunch all the last week Hamid, cringing in the
dark behind bulkheads, had beckoned me.into a cabin
where he had glasses and ice ready, a bottle of aniseed
pastis, and *casse-croûtes* of crusty flute bread with camem-
bert and frills of sweet pink ham. He knew my lunch in
fourth class would be stale and greasy, inedible: he
wheedled or stole his treats from the larder chef. He was
the first black man I'd ever met.

While I nibbled and made conversation he sat taut and
trembling. Then right there on the hot bunk he pounced
and spread me out and lay on me wriggling until with one
sharp squeal he subsided like a clockwork monkey. The
first time I thought he was having a heart attack; that's
what a sheltered life I'd led. He stained my dress. I kept all
my clothes on – a silken summer dress was all – and

clutched his curly grey head to stop him kissing me. He hissed. His wild eyes were red-threaded, his teeth furred green.

Through the port-hole came splashes and the squalls of birds.

By then – I would turn twenty in Tahiti – I felt that my formal education was complete. The day after my final exams I sold my textbooks to buy silk dresses. It was time for my *éducation sentimentale*. In theory, I knew what to expect. I had liberated views for those days – 1960 – and read widely. In practice I was a virgin; indignant young men had even called me frigid. (Was it true? Masturbation was a word in Freud to me.) But I had read *The Second Sex* from cover to cover in the original French. I had read Colette. I dreamed of becoming one of Colette's *grandes nonchalantes*, a *chère artiste*, a Léa. I wanted my defloration to be a slow and sensual, transcendant rite of passage. Where else but Tahiti, which was not only French, but Polynesian (I had read Margaret Mead)? I would be taught *le plaisir*, *l'amour*, *l'amour libre* – *libre* because untainted, there, by commerce or by force – in the tawny arms of a tropical man.

I was lucky. Tahiti would have remained nothing but a Gauguin daydream but for my mother's new lover, a bookmaker just widowed, who adored her. It was bliss and orchids every day, and champagne, French champagne, always there like a green cannon in its misty silver ice-bucket. 'This is the lap of luxury, Rosie,' she sighed. As a graduation present she offered me a fur, but I wanted a sea voyage.

'But darling, not on your own?'

'Mum, I've hitch-hiked all over Australia on my own.'

'But why Tahiti?'

'I can practise my French. Do some skin-diving. Please.'

'I don't know. I don't understand my own daughter. All this gadding around. I was a married woman at your age. Look at all the girls in your year that are married already or at least engaged. You've got an Arts degree, so what? You've still got a lot to learn. You're a worry to me, Rosie.'

'Oh, Mum, come on. It'll broaden my mind.'

'Well, I don't know.'

A few days out of Santo a telegram came from my mother: I had passed my final exams. NOW WHAT? she had added. That night I drank too much of the crude Algerian claret and sat on the rolling deck in a fever. Now what, indeed? Adventures on these high seas? A teaching job in Sydney? But first, Tahiti!

Là, tout n'est qu'ordre et beauté,
Luxe, calme et volupté.

That's a strange word, *volupté*. So is defloration, because it isn't like a flower at all, this female hole we have. Perhaps like a brown-fringed sea-anemone with a wet red mouth. Or a velveted clam. When the ship left, my mother gave me one long-stemmed rosebud that looked like withering before it could bloom. I held it to the tap in the cabin basin and pressed its red mouth open. Swollen red drops glowed on it as it stretched out sipping like a crimson snake. When my pubic hair first grew I stooped and peered with a torch and mirror at the coral frills of those lips ringed with whiskers. It is like a heart, its red folds and chambers. The membranes open like the petals of my rose, but shielded, husked with fur.

At our last lunch before Papeete Hamid grabbed my hand and offered to set me up in his apartment in Paris, in the Arab quarter. Was this *love*? But Paris! There would be weird drumming African music in the grey air, and the smell of baking bread and coffee; on the sky, those grey trees I had seen in so many films, scribbling themselves in the slow river, fading in mist. Rows of lights glistening in the boulevards. He'd be at sea a lot. Regretfully, I turned him down. Why did I? I might have been better off, who knows?

He didn't seem to hold it against me, anyway.

After all the passengers had disembarked and been through customs he sneaked me back on board and into the cabin. Gaudy girls in *pareu* dresses were sitting there, sipping *pastis* or ruby-red grenadine with ice. They were prostitutes of course – what other girls would Hamid know in Papeete? – with bodies like egg-loaves just out of the oven and tasselled black hair with a tongued hibiscus flower pinned in it.

I was taken aback at first. Prostitutes, here? Then I felt proud that Hamid believed that I was so enlightened I could chat with a pack of whores and never turn a hair.

'Hamid, *chéri*,' cooed one. 'She is *sensass*, your little *Australienne*. What are you worried about? I'll take care of her myself.'

Sensass was slang for *sensationelle*. Good. I wanted her to like me. She was fat and half-Chinese, paler, cooler than the others. Her eyes were the black enamel of a goldfish's under fine faint eyebrows. Her doll's mouth cooed broken French. Her name was Odile.

On the quay she waited smiling while I said goodbye to Hamid. I let him kiss my neck. Don't cry, Hamid, *chéri*, I murmured. I'll write to you. I promise. He pressed a wad of Pacific francs into my hand, as I had known he would, and he wouldn't let me give them back. I licked the tears from his poor red eyes while he whimpered in my arms like a puppy.

In the streets of Papeete women sat on the footpaths plaiting green baskets. At one end of the quay a replica of the Bounty was moored, looking too small to be real, as corpses and waxworks do. Her blurred spars and shrouds were winter trees twigged with yards on which her dusty sails were scrolled. At night she sat in a pool of oily light. MGM was making another Bounty movie. American extras with long hair swaggered along arm-in-arm with *vahines*, or slouched with them sipping beer in waterfront bars while Tahitian men glowered. Marlon Brando was said to be at large in this bar or that. All the footpaths said in long chalk letters: MGM GO HOME.

Odile took me to stay with her at her aunt's, in a big household full of women, children, ducks and black piglets with one ambling sow. It was one of a cluster of thatched and plaited *fares* with electric light but no glass in the windows, their hibiscus hedges draped with washing, on the outskirts of Papeete near a river and a black beach.

Those first long indolent days were filled with a hot, a golden light. We had nothing to talk about. We lay on sand that was the black ash of volcanoes, long plumes of palm shadow stroking us, and wrapped in *pareus* swam and wallowed in the still lagoon, twisting among bubbles, her gold body and mine still white undulating side by side. Fish slipped by, mailed and supple, trailing their silky fins. In the sunlit shallows they breathed dappled water.

'Rosie, you'll get burnt.'

'Will you put more oil on me?'

Her hands stroked the scented oil, *monoï*, on me, then mine on her.

Sometimes we fell asleep, waking with a hot headache, cross and surly. One afternoon a hot wind blew and the sand fluttered with the sound a wood-fire makes, burning us. Once a burly *vahine* waded thigh-deep with a net heavy with fish. Cats sat waiting at the waterline. The sky at sundown tightened and cooled on the sea like the skin on hot milk.

In the last orange light we had showers in the bathhouse with the ducks. We dressed up and brushed out our hair, songs on the radio, French and Tahitian. Odile taught me to dance the *tamure*. By the lamp at the window she put on mascara, white eyeshadow, lipstick. Arm-in-arm we strolled into Papeete, to this or that waterfront bar, Quinn's, Le Col Bleu, Bar Léa.

Once Hamid's money ran low, Odile was amazed, then scornful, that I refused all offers from men: not in the name of virtue, but of *amour*, of *volupté*. She was offended that my refusals pushed my supposed asking price up to five times hers. A white girl, a *vahine popaa*, was a novelty in the bars back in those days.

'Rosie, why not? After Hamid, he looks good.'

'After Hamid, who wouldn't?'

'*Et alors?*'

'*Non.*'

We both shrugged and pouted. I was not going to admit to virginity. Besides, I didn't like their attitude: that gross and condescending, sly black sailor plying me with wine punches, that silky Chinese millionaire, that rowdy Bounty extra. She soothed and cajoled my rejects, taking them in turn to a room she rented overlooking the quay. Most nights I walked home the long way alone.

Barefoot on the soft dust of the road I breathed the night's hot breath of jasmine and nectar under the stars. The hibiscus flowers were all curled up, all tightly folded. Strangers sauntered past talking, singing, plucking a ukulele: *bonne nuit, vahine popaa*, smiling at me. Sudden downpours of warm rain sent us all scattering with shouts and laughter to break off banana leaves for umbrellas. Afterwards the rain had washed a sweetness of strange flowers into the starry silence. Those flowers open only at night, Odile said once, pointing up, and then they wither at daybreak. No, that can't be true, I said. It's too beautiful. *Si, si!* She swore it was.

The first night that she came home at dawn I had lain awake all night, afraid. What was that pattering across the lino? Oh, a spider, Odile shrugged. Or a little mouse. She sighed, lying down beside me on the *pareu* bedcover, a Gauguin blue-and-yellow on the double bed her aunt had honoured us with. She was translucent as butter, so fat, so smooth, carved out of pale jade, my golden Odile. Her great breasts swung, blossom-tipped.

'I have borne a child,' she said. 'You can tell by my nipples, of course.'

Could I have? I wondered how.

'He is nearly two. My mother is raising him. They live on Bora Bora, where I grew up. Willy is his name.' She had a sad smile.

'Were you in love, Odile *chérie*?'

We girls in the bars called the whole world *chéri, chérie*.

'Love? No. Not with that one. No.' She looked side-long, those glossy eyes of hers narrowed. 'But now I am in love.'

'Mmm? Tell me about him.'

'He is American. In the Navy, the Seventh Fleet, I think it is. They were here on a visit last month. He lives in Hawaii.'

'Is he in love with you?'

She shrugged, and again that smile.

'Well, what's his name? Is he good-looking?'

'Yes, of course. *Sensas*. His name is Stéphane.' She took a letter from a mother-of-pearl jewel box by the bed.

'Oh, a letter! What does it say?'

'It is in English.'

Darling Odile,

Got your photo today, gorgeous. It goes everywhere I do. Wow, am I missing you! I can't get to sleep these nights thinking about how hot and wild you got me. We sure did have ourselves some good times! Honest to God, no woman ever made me feel the way you do in my whole life. What wouldn't I give to be sinking my you know what into that hot little Chinese pussy of yours this minute!!! I'm saving up real hard for your fare over here, honey, so don't you let me down now. Soon, soon, soon. I'm going to grab hold of you and eat you all UP! Write me, OK? French, Tahitian, Chinese, what the hell, so long as you write me, OK? The photo smells like your hair. Baby, words fail me.

> *Here's looking at you, kid.*
> *Steve.*

'I think he loves you,' I said.

'Ah, *oui*? What does it say?'

'Oh, you poor darling!'

I translated it. Tears of happiness rimmed her eyes with light. Mangoes when ripe have just that glow of red in their golden cheeks as Odile had. The sun was striking through the banana trees: I ran my fingers along her sumptuous breast and flank as daylight brimmed about us in the room.

'Sleep well, *ma pauvre petite* Odile,' I whispered.

But she lay stirring, sighing, for a long time.

Most mornings, while Odile slept in, I wandered round the market. There fish as tall as men hung from hooks by their horny lips, their huge silver eyes soaked in blood. I bought red and yellow bananas, and scented mangoes, and grapefruits with skins like pitted green balloons. Pale green flesh glowed in them. We always ate lunch at one long table with Odile's relatives: fruit and breadfruit, avocadoes from the tree, taro, raw fish. I learnt to make the raw fish, tuna or bonito, soaked in lime juice and coconut milk. Odile's aunt would never hear of my paying board, so I gave money to Odile to pass on to her.

At night if we were hungry we bought fried food from trolleys on wheels or ate *maa Tinito*, Chinese rice and red beans, in family restaurants with four or five tables, a basin on the wall, and one stand-up *cabinet* for everybody in the yard beyond the kitchen. Money was short.

That afternoon was stormy, not beach weather, so when Odile woke we went early to Quinn's. Sleepy girls drifted in from time to time and sat around gossiping, writing letters, lazily sipping beer. The band was rehearsing for the floorshow: the drums, the steel guitars, ukuleles, a hoarse baritone. The tables had a nap of golden dust. Between storms wet sunlight probed thickly through any gap into the languorous red glow cast by the stage lamps. Their crimson gloss coated all our hot skins.

I wrote postcards to my mother and to Hamid. I saw Odile's lip curl. Then we wrote Steve a letter in English. Odile dictated, and I embellished.

'Steve darling, I miss you too.'

> *Steve darling,*
>
> *I can't forget you. I remember everything about you, everything we did. It scares me to think we might never meet again. Tell me we will.*

'I shut my eyes and keep remembering how you made love to me. I dream that you're here beside me.'

> *I shut my eyes and keep remembering how it feels when you're inside me. I stroke you all over in my dreams, thinking*

you're here beside me.

'When they're lying on me I shut my eyes and think of
you. You're the only one I love.'

When they're lying on me I shut my eyes and think, oh,
Steve, Steve. You're the only one I love.

'I want to be with you. I'll come when I can. You
know I will. Trust me.'

I want to be with you. I'll come when I can, and we'll
make a new life away from Papeete. You know I'll come.
Trust me. My Australian friend Rosie is writing this for me.

'I love you, Stéphane, no, put Steve. Your Odile.'

I love you, Steve.
Your Odile.

The days that followed were too hot to go trudging to
the beach. After calling at the Poste Restante we walked
to the river instead. Beyond the ford of pebbles there was
a deep pool where we floated helpless as watermelons in
the churning, froth, our *pareus* billowing. We landed in
the shallows, thrown together, our bare skins grazed.
Once a snake lashed on the pebbles as I lay gasping, no, a
thick grey eel, then flickered away. Shadows arched in
the water. We were green–lit there like Gauguin's strange
white horse stooped to sip the coiled surfaces of water.

Once the whole family came with food in banana
leaves. We all splashed and dived, giggling. I heard
Odile's cousin, a sleek boy whose voice was breaking,
ask her something about me: I heard 'Rosie'. She replied
in Tahitian, grinning scornfully, and finished with a jeer-
ing laugh. Then she saw my face. Ah, *te voici*, Rosie,
where were you? She took my hand and waded to the
bank to plait out of leaves a crown for me and another for
her, and pressed them on to our dripping hair.

Was Odile not to be trusted? I dismissed the thought.

*

On my twentieth birthday there was a letter for Odile
from Steve at last at the Bureau de Poste, and a letter and a
cheque for me from my mother, with best regards from
the bookmaker. 'Wishing you many happies, pet,' she

had scribbled. 'How's my free spirit? Not too free, I hope! Thank your Odile from me, won't you, for looking after my girl. Be seeing you soon. Don't do anything I wouldn't do!' Of course, I hadn't written much about Odile in my postcards home, as she'd only worry. We cashed the cheque at the Banque de l'Indochine and went to Quinn's, where I wrote Odile a translation of Steve's letter.

> *Darling Odile,*
>
> *Just a short note to say I love you. You are just the sweetest juiciest woman I ever saw. You are. I'm sending you a little something by registered mail: wear it for me, baby. I mean, all the time. You promised. Write me again real soon, another letter like that. I can't wait. I can't get to sleep for thinking about you. I just want you like crazy the whole damn time.*
>
> > *Mad about you, kid.*
> > *Steve.*
>
> *P.S. Dear friend Rosie, thanks a million and keep up the good work huh?*

There was a photo too, of a grinning, heavy, broad-shouldered man, Polynesian dark brown, wearing a crown of leaves on a blue beach with coconut palms.

'What's he sending you, *chérie*?'

'The ring, I suppose.'

'The *ring*!'

I bought us a prawn dinner to celebrate, and later back at Quinns' we ordered French champagne. Odile was wildly dancing, laughing everywhere. Half-stifled in the crush, the smoke, I sat numb in an icy, foaming dizziness of champagne. A hot, fuzzy yellow light floated among the tables: in the aisles men of all races were crammed to watch the floorshow, Ruita on the red stage dancing the *tamure* to thudding drumbeats. I felt a nudge on my bare shoulder and, glancing, saw a man's black trouser-legs. Absurd to object. I sipped more icy foam. He rubbed gently at first, then harder and harder, until I heard a sigh above my head. My shoulder felt briefly damp when he moved away.

A group of Tahitian men from behind me, surging across, grabbed a table nearby: I wondered which of them it had been. One stared back at me with burning eyes. You? I thought. Are you thinking you've defiled me, using me? I tossed my head. You haven't.

The way home was long, dark, cool. My dazed head cleared. I watched the moon set, paddling in sand and the frills of waves among the many-breasted coconut palms, tripping in the starlight over coconut husks and the outriggers of canoes. A man with a ukulele fell into silent step beside me.

'*Bonsoir.*'

'*Bonsoir, monsieur.*'

'You like Tahiti, *vahine popaa?*'

'Oh yes, I love it.'

He was Tahitian, very tall, smiling with broken teeth.

'You are *Américaine?*'

'*Australienne.*'

He hummed a song, walking close, strumming his ukulele. The way home wound past hibiscus hedges, the *fares* here and there beyond them still glowing gold. At a bend in the sandy path suddenly his arm came tight round my shoulders. He dragged me stumbling through swordgrass to a banana grove. His ukulele fell with a cry.

'Stop it!' I gasped, clawing him. 'No! No! Don't!'

'*Je veux de toi.*'

'*Non! Je veux pas!*'

'*Je veux de toi.*'

He shoved me down in the rough grass, lifted my silk dress and wrenched my thighs apart. I felt him bore between my dry soft lips. His palm clamped down on my nose and mouth. Struggling, kicking, frantic for breath, I scratched and bit. He grunted, riding me the harder for it: he lunged and rasped inside me. Then his hand lifted. He shuddered, and lay limp on me.

When he got up three more men were waiting.

'Oh, please,' I begged him. 'Don't let them.'

He put his arms round their shoulders, muttering in Tahitian, but they scoffed and pushed him to one side.

The others watched, smoking, as one by one each man unzipped and lay on me, pushed his cock inside and thrust briefly. I shut my eyes. I was bruised all over, soggy and aching inside. None of them was brutal, and one who took too long was reproached by the others. I opened my eyes: it was Odile's sleek cousin. He was hissing, wet-faced. *E hoa*, moaned the others; get a move on, friend.

When it was over the three left me alone again with the first man. He knelt beside me, lifting my head, intent.

'*Ça va?* You're all right?'

I nodded. Then he did it to me again, riding my white body gently, his mouth – not his hand – over my mouth. He squelched in blood and semen, moving inside me. When he finished he straightened my dress and patted my torn, gritty hair.

'Go home, *vahine popaa. Va vite. Vite.*'

He slapped me on the rump, picked up his ukulele and went.

I cried, staggering home in the starlight, not daring to go and wash in the river or the sea. The tears boiled over in my eyes against my will. My teeth clenched on a child's whimpers and wails in the face of loss, injustice. No one saw me creep to the bathhouse or to bed. I told no one. They may have found out, I suppose. Odile may have known all along. There were no more late nights at Quinn's after that, no more night walks. I stayed in the *fare*, reading by lamplight, until I slept.

So much for my defloration. As for *plaisir, volupté*: they were lies in books.

*

In the shadows of our black beach I wrote one more letter for Odile. I did my best for her, though my heart wasn't in it any more. I mistrusted her now.

Steve darling, darling Steve,

I want to be with you so much, it's hard to wait not knowing when we can be together again. I think of you all the time. I think of how your hands stroke and hold me,

*and the look in your eyes then. I'm the same all over, but
you're all different colours, brown, russet, yellow, black. I
want to kiss you all over everywhere. I kiss that mole near
your left nipple, and the one on your thigh. Then – guess
where! I kiss the freckles on your nose and cheeks. Do you
like that? And of course I'll wear your little something
when it comes. I said I would, didn't I? Chéri, je t'aime.*

Your Odile.

*P.S. This is Rosie signing off and wishing you two all
the best, Steve baby. Sounds like you're real hot stuff!
Rosie.*

P.P.S. I'm blonde.

In a day or two my ship docked.

I'd been only vaguely aware of the date and the passage
of time until suddenly there she was: not the one I came
on but a sister ship, throbbing and glittering at the quay,
loading copra. I packed my bag and said my goodbyes.
We had one last day, on a white beach. Marlon Brando
was there with cavorting *vahines*. I didn't swim. I was
bleeding. I wasn't pregnant. I could see the ship's doctor
for VD tests. Coated with sand we ate slices of yellow
watermelon. The slanted black eyes that were its seeds
shone in its pale flesh.

I watched Odile roll in the sea. Sometimes in the cold
rough river, when her legs had tumbled apart, I had seen
the hairy blossom between them glistening. That, and
her lips, and her nipples, were the only red on her. She
was the same all over. How had she been broken in? How
had she borne it? Could she honestly love a man? The
memory was sour in me of thrusts and shudders, and
poor Hamid's soft squeals. Men are at women's mercy
then, the strongest men: wise women made the most of
it. My mother did. I should have asked Odile to teach me
her trade. A whore, she knew love's bitter mystery.
Odile *chérie*, I should have said, before it was too late:
teach me what I must know. Teach me pleasure.

In the chatter of the crowd by the gangway Odile hung
a mother-of-pearl heart on a chain round my neck and
hugged me, sobbing and sniffling. I knew I'd never see

her again. I went on board and waved to her. The ship's strung lights lay spindling in the water. A band was playing. In the distance the Bounty was a ghost ship. Long before we sailed Odile had gone. She was at Quinn's.

Jostled, I watched the quay drift away, and the lights of Papeete, and Tahiti's black towers of mountains hung with clouds. Thrown garlands of white flowers tossed in the wake. Stars floated. Eels were weaving in their dark caverns. I would sleep on deck to the twanging of ukuleles. Steve and Odile, I thought, the brown and the golden: soon you'll be heaving and coupling like the whales, the long sun aslant over you.

GERONTISSA

It has been another cold sunny winter's afternoon, dripping dead leaves in sodden gutters.

I see myself move through the shifting darknesses in these rooms like an amber glow, *une lueur ambrée*, in Melbourne, of all places. City of my birth, city of the dispossessed. I drowse, in this as in other rooms, like one already dead: an aura among shabby furnishings. My various faces evolve in mirrors downy with dust. Nowadays, I see, I am embedded in a mask of wrinkles, sprouting a white whisker or two on the chin, blotched with brown stains and magenta clotted veins on nose and cheeks. Shadows well in the ripples round my eyeballs. Age has congealed on me like wax.

In the lamplit street the sun, to my dim eyes, is splashed with waves of darkening blood, pale and drowning in blood. *'Le soleil s'est noyé comme un oeil qui se fige.'* No, that's not it. *'Le soleil s'est noyé dans son sang qui se fige.'* A yellow eye, an egg-yolk, blood-botched. I used to know pages of Baudelaire by heart when I was a young girl, even before I went to Paris. I stole my father's copy from under the musty shoes in his wardrobe to transcribe poems from *Les Fleurs du Mal*. I had it in Venice after his death and must have lost it there. At dusk along the back canals lights splash and dwindle, lamps in the windows of decaying tenements are lapped with water. Far below me lie shaken images of windows, as if in sunken basements. *Les bâtiments engloutis.* On a fretted bridge the shape of a woman dressed in black stands gazing at me with amber eyes.

For many years I have walked about my city alone, robed in drab black, passing for an old woman long before I was. I repulsed the eyes of strangers in the streets. Now I am embedded once and for all in old flesh, and crowned with a white frizzle on a pink pate, I who wore diamonds and pearls. One jewel I have left: a necklace of perfect amber. 'To match your eyes,' the giver said. It hangs like a cord of dry honey about my wattles, my blue-tinged dewlaps. It was a string of worry beads originally, a *komboloï*, dappled and lucent and more precious to me than any metal. It is none of your business how I came by it. I wear it day and night. I intend to go to the grave in it, if my last wishes are respected as they should be.

I had many lovers, some rich; and two husbands. Now I have mirrors on every wall and never dust them. My eyes have in any case been blurring lately. In sunlight they look to me as deep as water, flecked with green and brown. When I sit out in the sun, my eyes make swollen drops of dew flash in the grass with iridescent spokes and webs. Once a shower of rain drenched the heavy curtain of dust and sun. A rainbow spanned the sky.

I often sit by my window like this in the late sun, sipping Turkish coffee. I have an ancient primus in my room, against the rules but I keep it hidden. It is copper, with a cylindrical brass tank for kerosene, and burns harshly with a sharp blue flame. Laboriously I stir the sugar and the thick soft coffee in a small brass pot, more, I grant you, for old time's sake than for its muddy taste. Picture me sitting by my crusted window pane, ancient and massive, gowned in black, a tiny *café turc* perched in my bulbous fingers. I am quite aware of my absurdity. I make a note of it. I have not reached conclusion.

Gerontion, yes. You knew. I knew a lot of poetry by heart when I was a girl. I might be his female counterpart, *Gerontissa*, let's say, though no philosopher. I was a sensualist. No contact was ever close enough. I lived in Greece for a while and learned to speak Greek well: I was married to a Greek. He was the first of the husbands that I started to tell you about before mirrors distracted me.

Panagiotis was dark all over, and covered with black hairs. He had singed eyes like those of the Christ in ikons. I married him on impulse soon after we met, in the grip of a lust from which we woke exhausted every morning, wrapped in the damp sheet, still enlaced. We lived in his mountain village of whitewashed houses with lichen on green slate roofs. When autumn came we ate walnuts and glossy roast chestnuts by the fire, and sipped raw new red wine like a flame in the glass. Hidden in the fog all day donkeys minced clattering down the cobbled street, saddle bages crammed with chestnuts, to the *kafeneion* and beyond. The *kafeneion* was on a platform overhanging a cliff, high above the glittering port and the gulf. Great trees shivering in mist, an icy spring. Women, decent women, sat in whitewashed kitchens gossiping and embroidering by the *somba*, the stove; they couldn't go to the *kafeneion* in those days. After church one Sunday I dressed up in my husband's second-best suit, sauntered in among the dour men playing *tavli*, and ordered an ouzo. A silly prank, it was greeted with outrage. In our shuttered bedroom with its gold-leaf ikon Panagiotis tore his clothes off me, beat and then raped me. The marriage ended soon after in a miscarriage. I wrote to Anne to meet me in, of all places, Lesbos. Bravado, yes, why not?

I had many many lovers in my time, Anne, my darling. I had my share of pleasure. I resigned myself to solitude only when my mirrors left me in no doubt that I was old and ugly, though hale – praise be to God, as they say – and hearty still. Only my eyes stayed young and clear, too clear.

Now I remember the sun's red eye. *Un oeil sanglant.* Yes.

> *Où comme un oeil sanglant qui palpite et qui bouge,*
> *La lampe sur le jour fait une tache rouge.*

That must be the morning poem, though. *Le Crépuscule du matin.* My father, who was a Parisian born, once met Guy de Maupassant. My father taught me French from childhood and filled my head with visions of cobbled streets by gaslight and trees rusting in the evening mist. There were aunts and uncles, first and second cousins, all over France. '*Oh, notre pauvre Paul! Et c'est toi sa fille, ma petite?*' And in Ravenna was his rich old Zia Livia in her splendour. Anne was a second cousin on his mother's side, Anne who always wore men's formal dress, and loved me, and drowned. How my mind wanders these winter nights.

At the darkening window I rim my eyes with kohl, as I have always done. I prepare a face, a sur-face, looming at me in the pane, black-rimmed heavy eyes and bright red withered lips over my bare gums. I know it is absurd. All is vanity. I do it for the girl under the wax mask. For her sake, too, I pour wine from the heavy flagon, shake it into a glass. I always loved dry golden wine. It sinks into my belly like cold fire, and may well be the death of me one day. There are crueller deaths. I expected to attain ease and amplitude in ripe old age, a benign calm to suffuse my last nights, as sunlight and wine do the days. I have attained only detachment. Solitude.

I find it harder to propel my tremulous masses through the grey streets these days. The landlady gets me my bread and milk, bless her. My ankles swell. My hands and feet are always frozen white. Ills and aches and pains assail me. Indignant at decay, I totter home of an evening clutching a heavy flagon under the cold red sky.

I spend a lot of time in the Botanical Gardens. I go by tram. Autumn and winter are best, when the leaves drip on the lily pads. I love spotted lantanas and the pods and wet bronze leaves of the Moreton Bay figs. On my bench under a moulting willow I sit in a black veil dipping my hooked fingers and nose into my *petit point* bag for bread scraps. Black swans with red-striped faces emerge splashing and lumber up on their webbed toes to snap at my fingers. I am an old beached sea-lion clutching crusts. I am the Bird Woman. Grey pigeons cling with tiny claws to my arms and knuckles. They have a gloss of green and magenta on their necks, and their throats press soft and warm on my blotched numb hands. One sidles up my shoulder to peer avidly at the jelly of my eyeball. I shake it away. Gulls squall and hunch. There are great flurries of birds and flashing water. *Puissance et délire*. Sun-sodden, I drowse.

*

Nets drying like leaves on a far sea wall. The pull and suck of waves rolling the grey stones at the water's edge. The late sun burns heavy on tiers of stone houses, on the crenellated castle walls. We swim slowly through the shaking sunlit images: on the green pebbles deep below, our shadows are outlined with bubbles of light.

As I watch in stupor Anne sinks slowly twisting and dwindling down to the sea floor, her black hair strung like seaweed about her silent gaping mouth.

I wake jolted with such anguish that I cannot move. Anne, my darling.

Molyvo, on Lesbos. A clifftop town of grey stone houses, crowned with a castle. I remember a cobbled arcade of cool stone and wisteria. Mornings on the balcony over the hazed blue gulf, with Turkish coffee and red felt peaches, liquid inside. Clay chimney pots and a white bell tower. A yard with white cylindrical fretty cheeses, *myzithra*, drying in the sun, and greasy wool in heaps, dun, white, black. A procession passes, bearded priests in black robes chanting, swinging smoke from censers; a *despotis* in embroidered silks bearing in a casket encrusted with gold-leaf the skull of the patron saint. A rooster and his hens at moonrise sprawled asleep on a stack of olive logs.

While I slept on in the shuttered heat one morning, Anne drowned in that clear sea. Fishermen thumped her, roped and sodden, out of the *kaïki* on to the stone sea wall. I cannot accept death.

We had eaten the night before in a *taverna*, on a high balcony hung with lamps and pots of basil. The far lights of fishing *kaïkia* flitted and slid on the black sea. A rowing boat below us lit a lantern in the shallows. The black image of a man with a spear stood in the prow. High above the clear stones of the sea bed it floated, trailing instead of a wake the throbbing reflection of the lantern. A waiter brought plump sardines and whitebait, wizened olives and peppered white cheese glazed with oil. We sat in silence and munched coarse yellow bread, sipped the cold island wine, picked grey flakes from the corpses of sardines. White beads of eyes and tiny clenched teeth. Lean cats twined glaring about our feet.

We were quarrelling, and she wept. I had been to bed with a neighbour, a fisherman. All right, so it was true, but it meant nothing! I stank of him. Fish, petrol, tobacco, sweat. I was a whore. I made her sick. She never wanted to see my face again.

She walked out, then. I sat on alone to finish my cheese and olives and all the wine, to the last drop. The rowing boat in its pool of light had drifted to the far stone ring of the harbour wall, where it lay like a fallen moon.

*

I turn on the table lamp and sit in its glow watching a tomato, its golden seeds spilling; a dish of brown beans; wine pure as glass. Wine chills my mouth and throat. It calms my solitude. I munch cold glossy beans, a waxen lump of cheese, tomato slices, and sop chunks of yellow cornbread in the juice. Food is good, but wine is sunlight distilled. Wine is life.

I have been going through my papers these last days, rereading everything as I doze at my sunny window hour by hour, before I throw them away. I had kept letters, sheaves of poems copied in faded copperplate, Baudelaire, Yeats, Eliot, Rimbaud, Cavafy; old posed photographs and sketches; mementoes, dried flowers, cards; notes jotted in forgotten streets. These few pages are all that I intend to leave behind, as proof that there was more to me than cold flesh stiffening in black rags on a rented bed.

The dusty *odalisque* in oils hanging on the wall is mine. The landlady may have it, unless it scandalizes her. A keepsake from my Paris days, *une femme lubrique*. Immersed in the paint, she is still long, sumptuous and shadowed, spread along the bed as if congealed, and stroked by tongues of candelight. At her throat, an amber necklace. She has a nest of dark hairs above her thighs; a green bottle and a candle by her side. She sips from a flute glass.

I pour another glass of floating wine.

Marcel is dead, who painted it: and here am I. There is no one left who can remember me. I think he had little talent, and he drank and took drugs. I found him waxen and gaunt on the bare mattress, blotched with cold vomit, urine, blood. I sponged and dressed him, washed his stale clothes and hung them round the room to dry, cadged bones and bruised vegetables for soup which I spoon-fed him. *Une Garde-malade pour l'amour de l'art*. In the end I left him, taking the painting with me.

My other husband, Tom, a journalist, brought me back to Melbourne just before war was declared forty years ago. Then there were teas and date scones by suburban firesides. Picnics in the tea-tree. I remember tram rides to the wooden Baths, and the flat red bay at sunset aglow with wet street lamps. Tom was shot in New Guinea. I have lived on and on. I have been many women in my time. There is much I could remember. But to what purpose?

An old man I often see trudging about alone has a look of my Tom about him. He has long gingery-white hair down to his wrinkled collar, a rough grey beard, slumped tweed shoulders, notebooks sprouting from his pockets. From time to time he scrawls in one. Passers-by stare. I scrawl notes, too, hobbling in the windy streets – was Melbourne always so windy? – my memory being frail now. I wonder what he writes, and where he lives. I figure to myself his rooms, his stove, his wash-troughs, his bed. I look at the lights of shaded lamps hanging in windows.

*

After the war I sailed back to Europe and the ruined opulence of remembered cities. *Le sombre Paris*. I worked when I had to, in hotels, eating houses, bars. Exiled in this sagging flesh, slowly I felt my heart stiffen and grow old and brittle, tired of the complexities of love. I embraced solitude.

I have forgotten when and why I came home to Melbourne, of all places; and to this house. I have lived in this one room for so long now that I am bounded by it as if by an old skin.

My long sash window faces the sun. A grey net hangs over it, and dusty cobwebs draped in a festoon. I have nailed a sugar bag across at shoulder height, since I leave the ceiling lamp on all day and half the night; but the top pane is always gold. *Une lueur dorée*. All my mirrors glint with it, mirroring me. My floor is glossy wood, with a worn square of carpet. My walls are papered with brown cabbage roses. I have a wash stand with a flowered water-jug; a table, an armchair, a sofa bed with a patchwork quilt. On the walls, a nude in a gilded frame, and many mirrors. A wardrobe with an oval mirror in its door holds my black rags, my copper primus and flagons of wine, my coffee, honey, bread, sugar. The landlady gets my groceries, bless her, and brings me hot soups in her speckled saucepan. A kindly soul, but garrulous.

The bathrooms and lavatories here are a long way down the passage. I have a china chamber pot with rosebuds on it. Taking pains not to wet my hoisted skirts and the carpet, I squat my buttocks on its cold rim. In the morning I must stagger through the dark echoes of the passage bearing at arm's length my rippling chamber pot. One night a week I take a precarious shower in the slimy bathtub, soaping my loins and my scant pate and the nest of rough hairs under each arm and between my legs. My knees shake. Warm streams of water splash down me, lap at my knobbled feet. I hasten to dry and swaddle myself again. I must not catch cold.

I sip the last of the wine: my mind is burning. Carefully, immersed in the mirror, I take off the black rags that drape me. The necklace glows on my livid bones and cords. I am humped and gnarled. The flesh that hangs off these bones looks like paint that has peeled in webs over cracked plaster. How many of us pliant women, embedded like bees in the amber of our mirrors, believed we must come to this? I turn out the lamps. In darkness, crawl between cold sheets.

I am tired of living.

SNAKE

We are not told anywhere, are we, that winters in the Garden of Eden were not cold? The olive and the lemon ripen in winter and it could not be Paradise without them. Lemon and olive, sour and bitter, my mother would say: they suit you, Manya. Mama misjudges me.

I think as winter comes, why huddle here in three warm rooms? Why not go to Athens, say, and see Aunt Sophia? My dear old Aunt Sophia. Walk up to the Acropolis again. Order coffee and sit and watch the hollow city brim with a violet glow, and the lights and stars shine out. Sit on the cold stones of the theatre, high above its golden statuary, where I saw Euripides performed, Aeschylus. Or even go to Crete. It's sunny there. But I feel anxious away from here now.

Three years ago I went away. Mama and I went to the village in Macedonia when her sister Vasso died. As always when the ferry casts off in the crescent harbour of Mytilene I felt lost, speechless with dread. The Thessaloniki ferry passes between Turkey and Molyvo in the strait. I see Molyvo in the distance, its blue citadel. I never rest – those weeks in the frozen village, my God! – until we pass it again. So I might stay and see my olives through the press instead.

Aunt Vasso's own sons hadn't come down from Germany. Uncle Manoli, a dour man at any time, hardly spoke. After the funeral we were snowbound for silent weeks. I remember the full cheese-cloths hung high on black branches of the grapevine over his front door, their icicles of whey pointed down like teats. A wolf off the mountains howled at night. We cooked what we found:

macaroni, rice, icy potatoes and onions, eggs, my aunt's tomato paste and preserved pig from a crock deep in snow on the window sill. There was milk. We made cheese day by day and stored it in its crock in brine, weighed down with flat river stones. At night – from three o'clock, I remember, it was night – Mama and I huddled by the sooty *somba* roaring with apple wood until we succumbed in the stuffy dim yellow room to stupor and sleep. My uncle kept a horse and goats in the barn. An Arctic winter of darkness they lived through, shivering and crusted with excrement. He came home to milk the goats – we boiled the milk – and then sat in the *kafeneion*, glowing with ouzo, silent. The river froze. I had been there before, but in summer. Thank God I need never go again.

I keep busy all day in the garden, and at night I read. I paint a little and my work sells in town. It is not dull, just peaceful, in Paradise. And our green Lesbos is not like other islands. Lesbos was rich in art and poetry when Athens was a village and Thessaloniki still under the sea. They are as natural to Lesbos as her olive trees are, and we who love them are not thought eccentric here.

Still, I am thought eccentric. I am over forty and have never married. Mama has stopped her wailing over me and her tireless matchmaking. No man would have me now. Even Mitso the Idiot, who tried to rape me at a wedding once, would scowl and snarl at the thought now. As a girl I had no money, only beauty. That has gone. My dowry was my olive trees and the garden. Lemon trees grow here, pear and quince and apricot, peach and almond. We have red hens and a vegetable patch. This little house too would have become mine on my marriage, though my mother was left nothing else, as that is the custom here. Then my daughter's in her turn. I think Mama would be upset if I did marry. Not because of the house – she would stay here, of course – but because we make a good couple, she and I, whatever she says. We get on.

The first few times we saw Louka and my cousin

Dimitra in company Mama worried, sighed, watched to see how I was taking it. I have never told her the whole story. She guesses that, perhaps. Perhaps she even forgets now that I was engaged to Louka. She forgets my daughter. She fusses over them when they visit. She spoils their boys with sweets. It gives me no pleasure to see Louka. No pain either.

*

I was twenty when Louka came back from his army service to work in his father's restaurant in Molyvo. I was staying with my cousins there – Dimitra was still a schoolgirl – in their stone house at the base of the Genoese fortresss, the citadel on the hilltop. In the whitewashed sun of the chapel next door striped cats lay sleeping. We could see from three windows the stone arm of the port curled round its fishing boats.

Louka had always flirted. Now he came to the house so often, and singled me out so persistently and so respect-fully, that we knew he was serious. His mother called on my aunt to discuss the match. My cousins were thrilled. My aunt asked me what I thought. Yes, I said. The priest in his gold brocade came. We exchanged rings and were engaged.

It's hard to believe now what a passion I had for Louka.

He was beautiful, though, I remember, his hair so heavy and black when he let it grow, and his athlete's body dark brown and golden. After the rush in the restaurant he would sit with the tourists joking in scraps of their languages and put on music to teach them to dance the *sirto*, the *tsamiko*. The *zeïmbekiko* he danced by himself, his head sunk between his shoulders like a sated tomcat. He glanced at the women. Enthralled with Louka, they all clapped in time. There was ouzo, but most drank wine, yellow *retsina* from the barrel with its faint rankness of urine, of salt: as if the men treading it, unwilling to stop, let urine and sweat slip down their thighs into the must . . .

On still nights I could hear the *bouzoukia*. I lay awake.

When the music stopped, the restaurant was closed, Louka could come and whisper at my shutters. Shutters in Molyvo are solid, not slatted. I was a good girl, and shy. I wouldn't open them. *'Den m'agapas?'* he would growl, his voice thick.

'You know I love you.'

'Then let me see you.'

'I mustn't. I can't.'

'Come on, Manya, open the shutters, I just want to see you, just for a moment. Manya!'

'No. Go home, please. Louka, *please*. They'll *hear*.'

Some of those nights – or mornings, by then – he must have had Valerie with him.

*

She was not a typical tourist. Not one of the Europeans who descend in hordes to loll on the pebble beach oiling their bones or hire donkeys and ride giggling across the headland to bathe naked at the sandy beach and the hot spring. She was staying with some Australians who lived all the year round in Molyvo. But she looked like them. She smoked and drank and slept with men. She was tall and brown with lank yellow hair and a cat's pale eyes. Her nose and shoulders were thin, red under the freckles. What would a man like Louka want with her? So when friends warned me, I scoffed. Laughing, I accused Louka, but in fun. He tried to laugh.

'Don't look so guilty,' I teased.

Shifting and shuffling, he lit another cigarette and pleaded not guilty. I said I would call witnesses. I laughed as I scored this point but Louka leapt up.

'All right then,' he said. 'So it's true. So what?'

'You're in love with *her*?'

'Valerie? Don't be stupid.'

'Then – *why*?'

'Look.' *He* would not look. He breathed smoke in and coughed. 'I'm in love with you. You know I am. These others, they're whores.' These? How many? 'They won't leave you alone. I'm only flesh and blood, Manya, for

God's sake!'

'But, if you loved me, you couldn't –'

'Don't be such a baby!' He thrust his face close. To kiss me, I thought, and drew back. But no, it was twisted with feelings I could not read, of hatred, of desperation.

'Afti me gamaei.' She – makes love to me (so to speak). He bared his teeth to say it. Then he walked out.

*

I found Valerie sipping her morning coffee alone by the balustrade of a *kafeneion*, her eyes half-closed against the dazzle of the strait. She had no idea who I was. I sat at her table. 'Manya,' I said, pointing to myself.

'*Ego* Valerie,' she smiled.

'Louka,' I said, showing my gold ring and not smiling. She frowned. Her nose had peeled and her brows and lashes were white like cat's whiskers. She had a pocket dictionary. She looked in it and asked in broken Greek if I was Louka's wife. Not yet, I said, we were engaged, and found the word for her. She looked wise.

'Hmmm. *To paliopaido*,' she grinned. The bad boy. She shivered and picked up her towel. '*Thalassa*, Manya?' she said. *'Ela, pame?'* She really thought I'd go to the beach with her. She shrugged, grinned and flapped away down the steps. I was too amazed at the cheek of her to smack her face. I had expected to.

*

Louka, grown fat and bald, deceives Dimitra with tourists in summer – more deftly now, I hope – and with other men's wives in winter. Everyone knows. She will never leave him, though, nor he her. There are children, two boys: the elder a solemn bookworm, the younger a darling, a sparkling boy, and the children I do envy Dimitra. Nothing else. Sour grapes, Mama would say. No. Dimitra, each time she catches Louka out, attacks the woman. I, with my small experience, had more sense. She sobs and shrieks. She spat at one in the res-taurant, pulled another one's hair. Louka takes her home and humbly swears that she's his one true love. He's lucky he married Dimitra.

At the theatre once I saw *Agamemnon*. He had led grown men to the slaughter for another man's whore and for gold. So he was returning a hero to Clytemnestra, with his slave girl in tow. I have often dreamt since of her net and axe in the stone bath and Agamemnon quietly like a great fish pumping his blood through the water. She had a right to do it. He deserved death. Never for infidelity; she was unfaithful too. Death for their daughter's death. He led her into the trap at Aulis. I would strike the blow too, in Clytemnestra's place.

But not in Medea's. One summer night at a stone theatre cut into a hill among pines, the sky clear, the sea like milk, Medea writhed and growled for us and stabbed her little boys. For this she was raised in a god's gilt chariot and sat, the moon rising behind her, and gloated. Dimitra was there. It's whispered in the family that she holds this threat over Louka's head, should he dare to leave her . . .

When my Sophoula died Louka, I suspect, was relieved. He had never seen her. 'Who says I'm its father, anyway?' I'm told that he said. I prayed for Louka's death. I screamed to God for justice, of all things. I was mad for some time. I'm sane now and no longer pray or believe. I keep the fasts. I go to church with Mama. I eat the bread sopped in wine from the priest's chalice. God doesn't lift a finger.

Lesbos is close to Turkey. I have seen from the ferry people walking in the streets of Baba in Turkey as we passed between Baba and Molyvo in the strait. Our barracks and theirs are crowded with troops. The beaches are mined. We live in dread of another war. They do too. They love children, as we do. I believe that there is one thing that might save the world from destruction: our love of children. This is stronger than hate, or nothing is. This hope, or no hope.

*

Louka, when I next saw him after our quarrel, was at his most easy and charming, full of anecdotes about life in the army that convulsed my aunt and cousins. I was on edge, I remember. I had come to my decision. After the preserves and the coffee I stood and announced that Louka and I had arranged to meet friends at the restaurant. He looked stunned. Outside he asked me where we were going. 'Don't ask me yet,' I said. It was a sultry afternon, the whole town sleeping. I led him to the gullies past the olive grove where couples went. We lay on the dry grass.

'Now look. Manya, darling –'

'Take me,' I said quickly. 'Make me yours.'

'Do you mean it?'

'Yes. I want you. Take me now.'

He put his arms round me.

'Manya, not here. Not now.'

'Why not?' I cried despairingly. 'What's wrong with you?'

I didn't mean it the way he took it.

He pulled his shirt off, only his shirt. In the heat his body was rank and shone like varnished wood. The hair had stuck in curls round his dark nipples. He grasped me. Our teeth clashed and I shut my eyes. Tugging under my skirt, he lay on me and forced in hard and split my legs open. The pain, my God! I clung as he thudded on me. When he rolled away there was a sucking noise. He found a drop of blood and flicked it off.

'Louka?' I was close to tears.

'I hurt you. I'm sorry.'

'It's all right. I love you.' *S'agapo. S'agapo.*

Sighing, he lit a cigarette. Then abruptly he was on his feet. 'Cover yourself,' he hissed, and four boys, local children I think, burst on us there. They exploded into joyful whinnies and ran jostling and prodding to the beach.

'*Gamo to,*' Louka swore.

That was the first and the last time in my life, let the gossips say what they like. It was two whole days after it before I saw Louka. I spent them in bed pretending to be ill, but really ill, in a torment of shame and bewilderment. There was no one I could tell it to.

When he came at dawn and whispered at my window I – well, wasn't I his now? – I flung open the shutters. Appalled, Louka gazed up, swaying on the blue cobbles, Valerie clutched to him with one arm. She struggled free when she saw me, hissed furious words at him and clattered down the steps. I slammed the shutters. For a while Louka pleaded – those hoarse endearments of his – as if nothing had happened. Finally he stumbled away.

*

I didn't see Louka again for years. I left Molyvo abruptly to come here. I went for long walks alone and brooded. A broken engagement was shame enough to account for my misery, and Mama didn't pry. By autumn I knew I had to tell her. She wanted to hide me away with relatives – 'For your sake, Manya' – but I couldn't have borne to leave here.

I saw Valerie again that winter (winter, but the morning heat was heavy, very still and dusty, more like summer) at an umbrella-shaded table on the waterfront, reading. Drops of sweat glazed her red nose, her forehead and the sunbleached hairs of her upper lip. She looked up.

'Hey! Hey, Manya!'

I swung away, but she ran up behind me.

'Manya! *Tha piies kafe, kale?*'

Why not? I would have coffee. Her Greek sounded better. I nodded my ironic approval and she grinned, leading me back. The coffee ordered, we were silent, facing a sea that heaved and glittered at us. We made laborious small talk, what little we could. When the coffees and iced water came, she flicked through the little dictionary she still had and asked when the wedding was to be. 'Wedding?' I was as red as she was. Did she think me such a fool?

'Louka *s'agapo,*' she said. Louka I love you? She saw my face and tried again, pointing at me. 'Louka *s'agapo*

Manya.' She meant that Louka loved me.

'*Agapaei*,' I corrected. 'Yes? How nice.'

The coffee was strong and sweet and I drank the whole glass of water. In the thick sunlight her brown legs glistened with white hairs. Many Greek women are as brown as Valerie – I am white all over like cream cheese – but our body hair is dark. Some try to be rid of it; I never have. Those white-furred legs of her Louka had opened. Did he still? I wondered, but only dully. I was weary.

'Manya *agapaei* Louka?' she was persisting. I showed her my hand with its gold ring gone. 'Ah,' and she gazed with real regret. The Athens ferry had docked further along the quay and crowds with bags and boxes were hurrying there. She tipped small change on the table, picked up her bags – on one, I remember, swimming flippers flapped like an upturned seal – and jumped up.

'Manya, I must go, forgive me.' We say that when we go: she meant nothing more by it. '*Addio.*' Kissing me on both cheeks, wishing me luck. I felt too dazed and ill to speak. She looked back once in the surge of people to wave. I thought she gaped: perhaps she had just seen my swollen belly.

*

I had my baby in Athens and would not give her up. Aunt Sophia, our old Communist warhorse, was godmother and gave her own name when my mother refused. When I was well enough I brought Sophoula back here. For the evening *volta*, when families parade, I wheeled her along the quay in front of everyone. I suckled her a whole year. She walked at the age of one and swam at two. Before she had all her baby teeth she died of leukemia. I never saw a child to match Sophoula. Dying, she said 'Mama, where are you?' I was there holding her. I have worn black since that day.

It was God's judgment on my sin, people nodded. So may their sins be judged.

*

In this room my child and I slept: here I laid her out and waited with her for her burial. I often sit, as I sat then, at the south window and watch the sun, the moon, then the sun again. Having lived here all my life, I need its smell of paint, its floor of striped rugs, its dark points where at night the lamp will lay a gold hand on a cracked water-jug, three red stripes, a window sill.

Here in this room I painted Sophoula naked in her coffin, among pears and apples and grapes, a bunch of blue grapes in her hand. I drew in every detail of her: the ringed nipples, each crease and nail of her fingers and toes, the lips folded between her legs, her curled ears, her eyebrows with the mole under the left one. Had I been roasting the body on a spit my mother's horror could hardly have been greater, although, afraid of her mad daughter, she let me have my way.

'The pears are rotting,' was all she said. So they were, even before Sophoula was. 'Let the poor child have flowers.'

'It's not flowers that matter,' I seem to recall saying. 'It's the fruit that matters –'

'Is this what you will do to me as well?'

' – and death is the seed inside it!'

'What will become of us, Manya?' And she refused to sit up with me. I left her to receive the few mourners who came. My mother loves her visitors. I let no one in to see the child: my mother placated them. I sat alone with the candles and kept watch as Sophoula stiffened and then was limp again and her face changed. At first I talked to her. Then I brushed and plaited her hair. In daylight I painted her as she had become. Then I dressed and cover-ed her for the last time.

I have nearly all the paintings that I did when I was mad: all interiors with figures, as these were. Mostly they were self-portraits, mostly nude. The rooms in them are full of the whiteness that snow reflects, or moonlight; and so are the bodies. I have never shown or sold these. I can only look at them myself from time to time. I know they are here against the wall, as the dead are in the earth.

I know without looking.

I still paint myself nude. I have one on the easel now. It shows the blue branchings of my veins, the shadow of bones within, the slackness of my throat and breasts and swinging thighs – all my white meat run to fat, its tufts and wrinkles and moles. It shows everything. Still, it lacks what *those* had. My best work is in landscapes these days: watercolours done in precise detail. The parapets, yellow and violet–grey, of the fortress. Hills and their trees. The leaning figures in black of old women who mind goats. Children with shaved heads of brown and black velvet. Birds and insects and snakes. Old men lapped in shadow at the tables of *kafeneia*, sea light wandering on them as they drowse, these long afternoons.

*

Dimitra came to see me before she married Louka. I was fond of her when she was little, though I had not seen her since. I would never have tolerated such questions otherwise.

'I know you were engaged to Louka once. My mother –'

'What would your mother know?'

'I don't know.' She had trouble finding words. 'She doesn't know I'm here. She won't talk about you.'

'Good.'

'I've always thought of you as my big sister, Manya.'

'Have you? Why? We never see each other.'

'I always have. I wanted to be like you. Were you – in love with Louka?' Her jaw was trembling. 'Did he – why did you go away?'

'Pride. Ask *my* mother.'

'It's just that I – am I making a mistake? Should I really marry him?' At this point she hid her face in my shoulder. She was warm to hold. I stroked her plait of hair.

'Well, but you love him, don't you? You want to.'

'But will we be happy?'

'Sometimes. Why not?' She gazed with wet eyes. 'I hope you will,' I said. This was my pride speaking.

'Look,' I said then, and turned one of the nude self-portraits that I never show around to show her. 'What do you think?'

'It's beautiful.' She blushed and looked away. 'But you should have asked me first.'

'It's not you, Dimitroula.' She looked amazed. In fact it was exactly like her but for the eyes. Hers were, and are, like brown glass; mine, like green. 'Look at the eyes,' I said.

'Yes. But, Manya, even so – ' She was white now.

'I did it years ago. How strange life is! If I painted the eyes brown I could give this to you. As an engagement present.'

'No.' She shuddered. 'Oh, don't. No.'

*

At a friend's wedding once, when Louka and Dimitra were showing off their first baby, Louka clinked his glass on mine, leaned over and wondered in a hoarse whisper how I had stayed so beautiful. He said I was his one true love. He was, as usual, drunk. 'Darling,' he mumbled. 'Do you still love me a little?'

'To *our* child,' I said, and clinked his glass with mine, smiling even more sweetly. 'She should have been ten this year.'

He went back to his seat next to Dimitra.

*

Our garden is a few kilometres out along the flat coast on a lagoon full of seaweed and sandbanks. I hardly ever leave it now except to shop in Mytilene once a week. I love the crammed old shops that smell of roasting coffee, anchovies and cumin and olive oil. Skeins of late grapes glow there, withering, fermenting. At a waterfront table I sip my coffee, knee-deep in shopping bags. At twilight the harbour water is still. Darkness frills the images of boats at anchor and of sharp-winged gulls. Boys lolling on the edge fish among lights and stars.

I visit my old art teacher shivering in her frayed villa,

its tiles all tufts and nests, its windows cracked by a giant magnolia that is her pride. Excrement from empty swallows' nests trails down her walls inside and out. She is sitting for me. Children jeer at her gate and scramble to safety. 'Mad old Maria,' they shrill. Her eyes water. She turns off the table lamp to hide the tears. Maria is my name, of course: Manya, Maria. Is this how I will end, I wonder? A palsied crone mocked by children – I who love children?

My mother fears arthritis and angina. She fears death. Last year the village secretary wrote that they had found Uncle Manoli, her sister's widower, dead in the snow one morning. Mama was full of such grief, so many tears! 'Well, you have a hard heart, Manya,' she said. 'You won't even shed tears for me.' But what was old Manoli to Mama? No. It was just – Death.

Our life is calm. My companion, apart from Mama, is a cat patterned in black and white like a penguin. He lies breathing on a velvet sofa with his pink paws in the air. He is a shining seal; an owl when his black eyes shrink to gold plate with one black split from top to bottom and his blink is stern; a fanged snake when he yawns. He is everything in one, but his name is Fidaki, Little Snake. As a girl I once tried, from a sense of duty, to kill a snake I found writhing on my path. I threw rocks and silently the snake dodged, jerking and scraping, its gold eyes wild. All my rocks missed. Ashamed, I stood back and let it slide into a field of maize, its tongue touching ahead of it bronze clods of clay.

Maybe snakes hunt in our own garden, but if so I've never seen one. Fidaki himself hunts, but he is belled, the birds tease him. Mama said that Little Snake was no name for a cat. I said that the Garden could do without Adam and Eve, but must have its snake.

'Well, so it has. You are its snake,' she smiled. 'Yes, you are, Manya! Its fallen angel.' Smiling, but I could see she meant it.

PUMPKIN

'Just look at the men,' Barbara says, so Jill rolls over to look, brushing the sand off. Andoni and Marcus are loudly giving little Vassilaki a swimming lesson. Barbara waves as Andoni glances their way, but he fails to notice. 'When he's wet he looks like a copper statue. Or a glass one, filled with honey.' (Not like Jill's husband: Marcus is all bones and blisters.) 'Well, he does!' Because Jill has smiled. 'If you look carefully.'

Waving now as the two sisters sit up, Andoni passes his little boy to Marcus and dives under. Still with her smile, Jill watches Barbara wait until Andoni's black head springs up and shakes a spray of drops off before she will lie down again. Marcus is wading deeper with the boy on his shoulders.

'Life's good here, Jilly,' Barbara sighs.

'So I see!'

'I could live in Greece forever. Will it last, though?'

'Probably not.'

'But you keep smiling.'

'Not a crying matter yet.'

'You and Marcus? Problems?'

'Oh no.' Jill hesitates. 'Not really problems.'

'Then tell me: why probably not? Since you've gone all wise in your old age.'

'Not wise. Just old.'

'Not old. I'll be thirty myself in three years. Anyway, it will last. Andoni's mother tells fortunes.'

'God.'

'In coffee cups. I'm having long life and six kids.'

'You're joking.'

'Maybe not six. Five.'

'At least she must like you.'

'Yes. I'm one of the family.'

The shadow of a gull darts over the sand, sharp, more like a dipping swallow. Jill yawns. She rolls on to her broad brown back to brush sand off her belly. She looks like a beached seal, Barbara thinks. Jill catches her eye. They smile at each other ruefully. So much for having a *real* talk, the smiles say. But it is hot on the sand, watching the wallow and flash of the sun. Sometimes a wind ruffles their flanks and flickers away. The shadows of birds waver on them. Then the whole sky stills, as hot and bright as a ball of glass, and they are embedded in it. A searing din of cicadas numbs them. When they go in for a swim, the water pouring over them silences them; icy and deep, marbling them, making Barbara so white that beside her sister's tawny bulk she looks jade green. Their shadows reach out and touch on the sand of the sea floor: it is an illusion.

'Aren't you lucky you can tan?' Barbara has to huddle in the sand-crusted tent of her towel to save her skin from burning. 'You could pass for a Greek. I never will.'

'Not with that hair, no. Why should you?'

'Sometimes I'd like to.' Barbara shakes her head, scattering water drops. 'Vassilaki's lucky he's got Andoni's colouring. His big chocolate eyes.'

'Nothing wrong with grey. He's blond, anyhow.'

'Yes, but so was Andoni until he was six, his mother says. And his sisters too.'

'What does it matter? There must be blond and red-headed Greeks.'

'Oh, there are. Not where we live, though. They're all dark.'

'Dye your hair dark, then.'

'Mmm. Vassilaki's is going dark.'

'So long as you don't feed him on pumpkin!'

'Ha *ha*. They don't even have pumpkins here.'

It is irritating Barbara that Jill has harped on that old

joke since she got here; has even been calling her 'Pumpkin', as their father used to, having convinced both little girls that pumpkin turned hair that colour. She has always hated her hair. Now that it is going dark, though, she dyes it back: as if she were not Barbara without orange-gold hair that the sun turns to brass. (Has Jill guessed that she dyes it?) Andoni is proud of his wife's hair, there being little else to be proud of. Her skin is freckled; she is too tall, too thin. That is what they think in Greece: nice, but so ugly, poor girl. She smiles, watching Andoni and Marcus tow Vassilaki to the shallows. Strangers will take Jill for Andoni's wife, her for Marcus's.

'No pumpkins? What do you live on?' Jill is saying.

'*Other* things. What do you? They don't have passion fruit here either,' she goes on, because she has spoken too sharply. 'Dad's going to airmail me some from Australia.'

'Passion fruit?'

'Well, what do you think? Pumpkins? Look at Vassilaki.'

Marcus is tottering in the shallows with Vassilaki on his back. Everyone on the beach is looking. Marcus stands out as foreign even more than Barbara, with the grey-blond wisps of his hair flying and his face still babyish in middle age. He waves to Barbara and pretends to duck Vassilaki, who squeals. His grin is bracketed by long wrinkles. Barbara feels ill at ease with him. Have I forgotten how to talk to Australian men? she wonders.

'He's calling me "Auntie" now,' Jill says. 'And Marcus is "Marco".'

'He loves you.'

'Everybody.'

'You two especially. We're expecting you to go all clucky. Especially Andoni's mother.'

'Me? I'm not having any kids.'

'Why *not*?'

'Why *yes*?'

Barbara can hardly believe it. 'You were always saying you wanted lots of kids!'

'Oh, when we were little!'

'And after. Really, not even one?'

'Freedom before progeny,' Jill declaims.

'Have both. Well, why not?' She sits up with a squeal as Vassilaki squats dripping astride her belly. 'You're wet! You're squashing me!' He laughs. The men are calling, waving. 'Oh, let's go back in,' she says. 'It's too hot to talk.'

We're more like strangers now than sisters, Barbara thinks: it's been too long. Was it a mistake to come here? Jill is asking herself. Am I sorry we came?

*

Lunch at the *taverna* behind the sea wall is no different from lunch at home at twice the price, as Andoni's mother is always remarking. The same fritters of egg-plant and marrow; salad and *feta* cheese and olives; one platter of fried *sardelles* and one of various other fish in a tomato stew. The *retsina*, because drunk in the heat of afternoon, seethes in their stomachs and dazes them. On their plates flies and wasps stumble, drenching them-selves among sun-glossed bones and fish heads with white eyes. Listlessly Andoni's mother goes on spoon-feeding Vassilaki, until he baulks and runs off.

'Give the kid a go,' Marcus grumbles.

'It's a mother's duty to forcefeed. I'm falling down on the job. Not a good mother.'

'Stick up for what *you* think. They'll respect you for that.'

'Easy for you, Marco. You don't live here. Vassilaki! Stay in the shade! You'll burn, darling.' Andoni's mother looks sardonic. Vassilaki has climbed into a peeling canoe tied on the sand, and is struggling with the paddles. At last they jerk and thud. He looks up for applause.

'Mama! Baba! Marco!'

'*Bravo! Bravo!*' Marcus waves, grinning, and Vassilaki laughs. 'Let's get some more of this piss, will we?' He beckons a waiter dodging by with plates lined up both arms, but the waiter ignores him.

'Let's go home to bed,' Jill says. 'My head's bursting.'
It was she who insisted on making the long detour
through Greece to Barbara's fishing village. It seemed
such a good idea. She sighs.

'Come on. Since when did you take siestas? The
house'll be like an oven.'

His gesturings have caught the eye of the *lantziera*, the
old kitchen woman, and she stands up scowling
anxiously, her short grey hair on end. Every afternoon
she sits crouched over a bucket in the shade of the pine
trees and peels potato after potato, making potatoes roll
and bubble in her cold water. Now she gapes as this bald
Anglos mouths '*Retsina*' and jabs at the empty bottles. At
last, her toothless face showing a slow enlightenment,
she stops the waiter for them. Sullenly he brings a bottle
and opens it.

'*Kaka*, Mama.' Vassilaki is calling.

'Is that what I think it is, Pumpkin?'

'Oh damn.'

Vassilaki is squatting in the shadow of the canoe,
gazing round at the brown pile he has deposited in the
sand. People at other tables, their voices blurring, turn to
look. Barbara unsticks her elbows from the plastic table-
cloth to hurry down and wipe his bottom. Redfaced, she
wraps the soft mass in the tissues and crams it into a waste
basket. '*Ochi ekei*,' she scolds. 'Not there, little one. You
know that.' He smiles up. She carries him back and sits
rocking him. '*Nani*,' she murmurs. 'Sleep.'

'*Oriste*,' booms a proud voice. The old woman has
hobbled to their table.

'What's up?'

'She delivered the goods.'

'Did she? So she did. Good on you, Madame. *Bravo*.'
He nods to her, pouring *retsina* into all the glasses except
Andoni's mother's; she has her hand over hers. The
kitchen woman is tremulous with joy at the word
'Madame'; and now the *Anglos*, before anyone else
notices, is pointing to a clean glass and raising his white
eyebrows at her over his mirror glasses. She licks her dry

lips, and he fills the glass.

'Oh no,' mutters Barbara.

'Snob.'

'I'm not. We'll never get rid of her now.'

'*S'ygeia*,' says the woman. '*Marigoula*.'

Marcus cocks his head. 'Cheers,' Barbara explains. 'Her name's Marigoula.'

'Cheers, Marigoula. Bottoms up.' He and Marigoula drink. 'All, all. *Bravo*, Marigoula!'

She puts her empty glass down. '*Xenos einai*?' Giggling, she chooses Jill to ask. Jill shrugs.

'See. They all think *you're* Greek, Jilly.'

'*Nai*,' Andoni's mother suddenly says: yes.

'*Anglos? Germanos?*'

'*Afstralos*,' Barbara says.

'*Aah! Xereis kai milas? Bravo!*'

'Now what's she on about?' says Marcus.

'Pleased I can speak Greek.'

Families at other tables are watching, amused. Andoni glares at Marigoula, who smiles, raises a knotted arm to expose the wet grey tuft of her armpit, and fingers a curl of Barbara's hair. '*Oraia mallia*,' she croaks. '*San chrysafi. Megalonoun?*'

'My hair. Beautiful, like gold.' Barbara makes a face at Jill. 'I think she's asking if it grows.'

'If it *grows*?'

'She thinks it's fur. She's not the full quid.' To Marigoula she miaows and says, '*Ti nomizeis? Gata eimai ego?*' Do you think I'm a cat? At which Marigoula gives a delighted snort and pokes Barbara's shoulder. Vassilaki stirs and grasps a fistful of hair.

'*Mallia*,' he murmurs.

'*Ta vafeis ta mallia sou, kale?*'

'*Mi*.' Barbara shoves away the heavy cold hand.

'*Now* what?'

'She wants to know if I dye it?'

'God. Do you?'

'Well, sort of. I do use a blonding rinse. Sometimes.' She sees Andoni make an angry grimace at his mother.

Vassilaki wriggles, hot and heavy, his white eyelids flickering.

'Well, say so and be done with it.'

'Say you ate too much pumpkin when you were little,' Jill says.

'She wouldn't get it.'

'Try her. What's pumpkin?'

'*Kolokithi*.''

'*Kolokithi* – right. "Eater"?'

'*Troei poli kolokithi*.'

'*Troei poli kolokithi*,' repeats Jill with a grin. Marigoula's jaw falls and she stares from one sister to the other.

'Don't be so stupid,' Andoni snaps.

'It's just a family joke,' says Jill.

'Not this femily.' He jabs at a soggy slice of fried marrow. 'She think you want – thet.' Marigoula's eyes go round. With the grey nail of her little finger she is picking a scab on her neck; but the blood distracts her only for a moment.

'What? The zucchini?' laughs Jill, patting Barbara's hair.

'Same word.'

'*Kolokithi?*' crows Marigoula. She turns to Andoni's mother, who frowns and looks away. '*Ti leei touti?*' What's she saying?

'Jesus,' moans Marcus, pouring the last of the *retsina*.

'Well, you started it!'

'Right. I'll finish it. What the hell's "yes"?'

'*Nai*.'

'So what's "no"?'

'*Ochi*.'

'Right.' He stands up. '*Nai*,' he says loudly. Marigoula flinches. '*Nai, nai*. Now piss *off*.' And she totters gasping back to her bucket where she cowers, open-mouthed. 'Right. Everyone had enough? Well, let's go, then.'

They trail behind him up the sullen street with all its shutters tight against the sun. Andoni stalks beside his mother, his fretful little boy swaying on his shoulders, hands clamped in his father's hair. Jill puts an arm round Barbara's shoulders with a grimace of sympathy, but it is too hot to walk far like this. Their clothes are sweaty and prickle them. She lets her arm fall. No one speaks until halfway home Marcus lets Andoni catch him up.

'Game of chess, mate?'

'I want to zleep.'

*

The shutters of their room are fastened, but the window panes are spread wide open, back against the walls. In one and then the other she sees her dim reflection. A white shape, a clown's bright wig. She kicks off her sandals. Her arms and legs are rough, speckled with sand. The sounds of splashing and little squeals come up from the yard: Marcus and Jill, hosing each other down. Sand goes trickling under her dress.

Andoni is taking his time.

She hovers over a half-eaten bunch of grapes in a bowl of water on the table. The stalk is curled over the last grapes like a scorpion striking, branched legs thrust out. When she touches one black grape, a blowfly she has not seen on the stalk jolts away. She springs back. Sizzling, it blunders here and there against glass, thudding now on to the framed mirror, now on the panes. She pads over to unfasten the shutters and it is like walking on sugar.

Andoni walks in, shuts the door, and lays Vassilaki, washed and dressed and asleep again, on to his white bed. 'Mama?' he murmurs. Andoni tucks the sheet under his chin.

'Don't open them,' Andoni says. 'Is too hot.'

'There's a blowfly. *Vromomyga.*'

'Where is?' Andoni grabs her exercise book, gazes, and slams the heavy fly against the wall. 'I get her.'

'My book!'

The fly's crushed black panels have oozed a cream of eggs on the red cover.

'Sorry.' With a fingernail he flicks it off the book on to the floor. 'It come off. All right?' With a disgusted glare she grabs her book back; he stares back coldly. 'You come to bed?'

'I'm all sandy.'

'Me too. Doesn't matter.'

Their bed is made up with coarse hand-loomed sheets. On a small table beside it, with the necessary cross-stitched cloth, they have a glass of water, the black grapes, a cup full of pens and pencils, the red exercise book with its dark smear, and a folded newspaper, TA NEA. But Andoni is not going to read. He is already in bed with nothing on but his dry bathers. She rasps her sandy soles one against the other and slips in beside him. He lies still. Silently she picks up a pencil and her book.

'You *hev* to say you paint your hairs?'

'Why not? Since I do.'

'You hev to say to everybody.'

'Why not?'

'Because thet old woman ask you, you hev to say?'

'Marcus said.'

'You say first.'

'Oh, Andoni. She's simple-minded, poor old Marigoula. What does it matter?'

'Other people listening too. Aren't you shame?'

'No. Sorry. Should I be?'

'You should be proud?'

'Oh, that's enough! Leave me alone, I'm tired.'

'You mek fool yourself,' he says, 'and me too.'

'How come?'

'Womans never paint their hairs here. Not good womans.'

'I've seen plenty who do.'

'No.'

'Let me tell you. Your own sisters in Thessaloniki do. I've seen it in their bathrooms. It's no secret.'

'So?'

'So. Some good womans do.'

'If they do, they shut up about it.'

'Good on them. Why don't *we* do that?'

She turns her back and drags the coarse sheet up over

her head, which feels bruised from the wine and heat and unshed tears. Vassilaki cries out once, and sleeps on. She watches Andoni's dark face breathing deeply, until she is sure he is asleep, her copper Andoni; then creeps out on to the balcony. The sun has just swung on to the gold wall of their room with its shutters clamped.

'You tired or what?'

She starts and turns. 'No.'

'You say you are before.'

'I'm not now. I want to catch up on my diary.'

'Tomorrow.' He reaches for her arm, but she moves. 'Come back.'

'No. I never have a free minute. I'm sick of it.'

'Oh. This is new. I see. I see.'

'I really don't *feel* well.'

'Don't give me that shit.'

'I *don't*. Leave me alone!' She has spoken louder than she meant to. Andoni pales. Jill's door opens suddenly and she looks out, puffy and tousled.

'Pumpkin, what's wrong?'

' "Punky"? What is?'

'My old nickname. My – *paratsoukli*.'

'What's for this name?'

'Oh, my hair of course. My bloody hair!' Barbara holds up tassels of it. Another door creaks: Andoni's mother, gazing, shocked. Andoni swings round to Jill.

'Is time you go,' he says. 'You only mek trouble for Varvara and me. First time this happen.'

'They'll stay as long as they like!' Barbara can hardly breathe. 'Jill's my *family*. My flesh and blood!'

'Not mine,' he says. 'I'm the bloody boss here.'

'So *what*!'

'Look, calm down. It's all right.' Jill's voice twangs. 'That's fine with us, Andoni. Is tomorrow morning okay?'

'Is okay.'

'*No*! You only just got here! After all these years and years!'

'It's not working. He's right, it's hopeless. Look, we'll

keep writing. Won't we? There'll never be time for a *real* talk now.'

'Tonight?' Barbara whispers.

'You're *jo*king!'

'Please.'

'I know: come as far as Athens with us! Just for a few days. Oh, come on, you'd love it. You said you'd hardly seen Athens!'

Barbara glances: Andoni's face shows nothing. 'How can I?' she says. 'What about Vassilaki?'

'Vassilaki too, of course.'

'No,' says Andoni. 'Sorry. Not Vassilaki.'

'I think, some other time, Jilly.' Barbara forces a smile.

'You see?' Jill shrugs. 'That's progeny.' She pats Barbara's cheek and without another word goes into her room; they glimpse Marcus's sleeping head, before the door closes. Andoni's mother closes her door. Andoni stares at Barbara with twisted lips. Then he walks into their room and slams the door on himself and the child.

SUMMER ON ICE

The first time Caroline goes skating the cold shocks her, such motionless cold and in summer. Her breath fumes. The building, a hollow barn she remembers from her childhood, is uglier, darker, older than ever. Long drops of water fall from the ceiling to make blue lumps on the ice. She has been imagining ice like deep glass, bluish and with long needles of air frozen in it, but no: it is frosted, slashed and scarred, although no one else is there. A net hangs behind where the hockey goal was last night. She regrets having come.

A grinning boy hands her a pair of skates. She laces them tight as she has read she should, and clumps to the swing door, on to the ice. She slithers, clinging with both frozen hands to the fence to drag herself along. Her feet sting with the cold then go numb. After a dogged hour she can propel herself with one hand. No one else has turned up. Records of rock songs boom now and then over the loudspeakers. A cone of sun burns through a skylight. Dark trees flicker at its glass. When there is no music her skates scrape and thump and she remembers how her skis thumped on the hard snow of a sunlit mountain top the first time she dared go so high; her terror then as she crouched curling down and down.

She prances out of the rink on suddenly light feet, pleased with herself. The bay is opaque olive green this morning. Yachts on it flutter their wet sails. In the haze of the western shore, the towers of Melbourne are grey slabs, tombstones. In a week it will be Christmas.

*

A scrawled postcard in her letter box, the first: the Statue of Liberty and a New York postmark.

> *My darling,*
> *Remember how we lay and drank champagne and dreamed of being here together? I miss you terribly — a million things to tell you. Found you some books you'll adore in the Gotham — not telling what — and mailed them yesterday. They should arrive soon after I do, some time in mid-Feb., I hope. It's freezing here . . .*

He gives the address of a post office in Greenwich Village where she can write to him, and signs off: '*Take care, sweet.*'

*

Has he remembered that they quarrelled then as they lay and drank champagne? He hasn't, it seems.

'I wish you were coming with me,' he murmured.

'Well, I would. I could afford the affair.'

'What did you say?'

'The fare. I could afford the fare.' They both laughed.

'Will you wait for me, Caro?'

'Oh, probably.'

'Eight weeks.' His eyes were fixed in anger. She sat up.

'All right, it's not eternity. I know. Eight weeks is eight weeks – of jaunts and sensual joy in the Big Apple while I sit waiting.'

'It won't be joy. I'll be thinking of you the whole time. You know that.'

'I'll think of you.'

'Promise you'll wait?'

'No! What gives you the right to ask?'

'Caro, listen. I can't not take her. She's been looking forward to it all year. All our friends know we're coming over. I can't *do* it to her.'

'But I don't *want* you to. Have I ever said I did?'

'But you won't wait?'

'Won't promise to. I can't. On principle I can't. It's something time will tell.'

'I see. Yet another of those somethings of yours that time will tell.'

'Yes. Like: "I told you so." '

He started to dress, talking over his shoulder.

'You claim to love me.'

'Yes. Not the point, though, is it?'

'I think it is.'

'You love me, you claim. You're going with her.'

'She *is* my wife.'

'Yes. *That's* the point.'

'I'm coming *back*.'

'I'll be here.' She shrugged.

'Will you? Alone?'

'As far as I know.'

With a gasp of anger he walked out. She cried, but noticing he'd kept his key she didn't lose hope. The next day she sent (to his work address) a card with a Pre-Raphaelite Ophelia afloat in skirts like a peacock's tail, on the back of which she had written: *'Look in my face; my name is Might-have-been. (D. G. Rossetti – SONNET 98)'*. On the third day he came. They lay in bed all afternoon and listened to a broadcast of the New World Symphony. He promised they'd live together when he got back. She promised to wait.

*

Against her will, as one who prides herself on being free of possessiveness – relatively free – Caroline imagines him arm-in-arm with his wife, a jolly figure though faceless, strolling along Fifth Avenue. Caroline has never been to America. She buys a book of photographs of New York and studies the sunset skyscrapers, the squirrels and snowdrifts of Central Park, slums in the Bronx on fire. In one photograph a small tree of grey twigs on some avenue is spun all over with webs of white lights, for Christmas, she thinks. Has he seen it?

She finds a photograph in her book of a man at a block party in the Village, swaggering on a stoop, thumbs in his belt and his curled chest bare. A glass of beer in one fist. His stance, though not his face, reminds her of her lover and she puts a marker at that page. Soon the book starts opening there of its own accord. She takes the marker out.

Am I compulsive? she writes in her diary. Am I old-maidish? I'm thirty-two. Am I becoming a tedious woman? I was never so mild and quiet, such a mouse. Be fearless and joyful. Make him love me.

She takes over her sister's flat near the beach. Her sister is working in Sydney. Packing and scrubbing out the old flat and moving her things keeps her too busy for a couple of days to feel lonely. She has told him her sister's number but no calls come. Is he trying and not getting through? She writes to him about the flat, Poste Restante. What, she worries, if in a new flat she seems like a stranger to him? She does to herself.

*

At last he rings her from a coin phone in Manhattan in a downpour. For her it's another sultry Melbourne night. They spar and hedge, off-key, and say nothing in the end.

'I do miss you, Caro. Really.'

'Oh, good. Now and then would be nice.'

'All the time. Was that a laugh?'

'A cynical snort, more like it.'

'Undeserved.'

'Is it? I miss you too.'

'Good.'

'Darling, it's four in the morning! If I'm not making sense, make allowances.'

'I wanted to catch you in. I hoped you wouldn't mind.'

'I don't. You're sure of your welcome.'

'Actually, I'm not. Far from it.'

'You always seem sure.'

'It's the best policy.'

'Better than honesty?'

'Much.' He pauses. 'You seem sure yourself.'

'I do? What do I seem sure of?'

'Me, for one.'

'Baby, you gotta be kidding.'

'Well, you can be.'

'Yeah?'

'Hey, I'm the one should talk American. Yeah.'

'Put it down to my sceptical nature.'

In no time the three minutes are up. She lies on her bed with the lamp on, wishing she had let the phone ring. He is standing bitter in the rain now, he who hates rain. She has lost ground, and lies wondering with a chill of panic if she has ever believed that he loves her, and what does a married man mean by saying he loves her? Anyway.

*

Anyway, darling, the flat's in a narrow street with a little yellow-grey Gothic church at one end and at the other is the bay. From the balcony you can see right across. Now and then today a shifting wind has been blurring the sea. Then it comes still and clear again as if a glass dome had been put back on. The façade of the old baths is intact, and the one domed white turret that I can see from here looks like a whitewashed chapel on some island. Mykonos, Ios. In the evening I lie getting brown on the sand. I hope you like your women brown? I eat down there and before I come home sow my handful of crumbs although only one gull is even in sight – far out at sea, circling. In a long swoop it comes crying and others follow and stalk around. They arch their grey wings like scythes, ruffle themselves and jab the sand.

The lights go on in the city and along the bridge – a sudden golden bow. Freighters at sea flick on their white lights.

I close the French window and see my room move with the glass across the darkening sea and sky: a yellow lamp, a table with books, a chair on a white rug.

*

The second time she goes skating the lights and the plant have been turned off. No one is there but two boys cleaning up. Water swills glittering around the blades of her skates. She wavers, anxious not to fall and be soaked, so half an hour passes before she lets go of the fence. She hovers over the hockey circles, trying to balance on one foot at a time but never daring. There is music, then the needle sticks and it is switched off. The two boys circle, sweeping off the ice. She imagines him, back from New York earlier than he said, coming here to find her: herself catching sight of his smile of admiration and pride. She will be gliding, whirling in her mist of breath, in the spotlight that the sun makes falling on the creamy ice.

'You'll fall flat at his feet,' she says aloud, amazing the boys. Her laugh echoes.

*

After the turkey and Christmas pudding at her mother's farm, the family goes on drinking in the garden while she and her mother wash up. This year, though, they leave the dishes to soak, and walk to the apple orchard. Her mother is worried, Caro can tell, and wants her to talk about him. What is there to say? As she talks on, her mother breathes sunlit smoke; watching it, not Caro.

'Is he going to leave his wife for you?' she interrupts.

'Only if she consents,' says Caro.

'Consents? Oh, Caro darling! You and your dream world!'

There are days when Caro does feel as if she is living a dream. She is not real; or she is fading, becoming invisible; or is left behind by time. She lies awake all night. No one knows that they are – were? – lovers. Are we? Were we? she wonders.

*

Another postcard, the Chrysler building this time.

> . . . *So you're learning to skate these holidays, my darling? There's an open-air rink here at the Rockefeller Centre. Center. Some of the skaters are serious and waltz eyeball-to-eyeball as in their young days in old Prague and*

Budapest. The young guys clown around pretty girls in tutus who loftily ignore them. Lovely to think of my darling in a tutu. Had any falls yet? Take care, as they all say here. I love you . . .

He mentions that he has been to see a revival of 'West Side Story' on Broadway. He always writes 'I' not 'we'. She is reminded of one morning when, arriving unexpectedly, he found her still in bed and joined her there and later got up to make coffee. Naked at her little stove he swayed and sang 'I feel pretty', a cigarette dangling. His smile when she laughed was full of innocent bafflement. She wonders if he was reminded too: he doesn't mention it. She tries not to feel hurt.

She writes in her diary: *Is he thinking, poor little Caroline, writing his postcards?*

Caroline, stop it.

*

Caroline has started indulging in exotic foods. Am I trying to sublimate desire? she wonders. She buys a smoked fish in its cloth of gold, sullen-mouthed and swarthy. Creamy avocadoes in coarse black shells. Pumpernickel like sour plum pudding. Cheese crusted with black peppercorns or riddled with blue mould in crumbs or dimly veined with wine. A round Edam in red wax like a toffee apple. She eats her cheese with morello cherry jam by the saucerful. She buys quantities of Turkish coffee and tart Chianti in straw. At one sitting she eats a whole jar of peanut butter. She bakes a tray each of pumpkin and sweet potato in the oven of her new flat, filling it with smoke in which lurk the ghosts of other tenants' burnt dinners, her sister's probably. In reaction she eats nothing for a week but fruit: mandarines with spongy skins, bananas and sour early apricots and plums. She buys a glossy oval crimson fruit which a poster in the shop names a tamarillo. It looks like the glowing eggs baked into plaits of bread in Greek shops over Easter. Cut, it is orange, studded with dark seeds in a butterfly shape. It tastes of passionfruit and pawpaw together and

Caroline savours every bite. The tamarillo, she reads, is a winter fruit.

She takes herself off to various good restaurants with a book and a half-bottle of fine wine. She reads *Pale Fire, A Lost Lady, Washington Square*. She orders Chicken Maryland, Manhattan Clam Chowder, Pastrami, things he must be eating. She is a slow eater and a fast reader. She keeps her head down. She hopes people are not looking at her in sly amusement.

> *I'm not a bold person*, she writes in her diary. *Not an innovator or a rebel. Not the life of the party. But I am self-sufficient and don't much mind if strangers patronize me.*
>
> *He'll forget me. Worse, I'll seem drab and dull when he gets back. I listen to concerts recorded in San Marco's in Venice, in New College, Oxford – places I've been to – and wonder how my life can have shrunk so small. Someone vivid will catch his eye. He'll drop me.*

In an Italian restaurant she eats little sea creatures stewed in wine and tomatoes: whole baby squids and mussels, scallops, shrimps and clams tangled on the plate in what looks like red seaweed. She drinks her green Italian wine. It is raining, a summer storm. From her window table she sees puddles begin to swarm with rain. Restaurants in New York have glassed-in verandahs like train carriages flush with the footpaths. She has seen them in her book. She imagines she is with him inside the golden glass of one of them, rain shivering down it and people rushing past, heads bent, smiling in at them from a black and silver Manhattan street. The waitress brings fruits, grapes and peaches and watermelon, unasked with the coffee. He said so in a letter. A candle, she thinks; a bowl of autumn fruits, a green bottle; our hands clasped on the red cloth. Afterwards, running home in this rain. No. On iced footpaths, sidewalks, slithering, hand-in-hand, our breath white: like skaters.

*

The third time there is a mist over the ice. Two other women are there practising leaps and figures. They smile sympathetically at Caroline's wobbles. The sunlight is a bobbin wound with gold mist and, dazzled, she can easily imagine that she is not here but in Central Park. Or the Rockefeller Centre. Center. In a letter he has mentioned smoking pretzel carts and puffs of steam from under the streets like white balloons hovering; or on a windy day flung shredded between glass walls, fluttering in the mirrors the walls make. She weaves – but in blue jeans, not a tutu – through the mist. She will amaze him at the Rockefeller Center one day, one day.

After two hours she can go round and round the rink quite fast without ever holding on and the two women smile and say how well she's doing.

*

He writes a lot. He writes, for example, about the hotels he (they) stay at, in rooms on the thirtieth and fortieth floors. 'Like in a helicopter, a huge ferris wheel. You sleep among stars.' She imagines him (them) high up at the summits of glass towers all gold and silver light, webbed with their long lamps and hung among stars. To make love up there, she dreams, though heights freeze her with terror. And what if they sway in the wind? She goes to Luna Park and grimly rides the ferris wheel above the glittering city.

Then he writes that he's moved to the Village now, to a friend's apartment.

> *Greenwich Village has all these red tenements caged with fire escapes. Basement rooms with lamps on all day. You've read* Washington Square, *haven't you? I was there today. The fountain was empty, just a skin of grey water and dead leaves. A pale boy was sitting on the rim gazing in, his feet bloated, red raw. I've never known such cold. You must have in Europe. There were trees, lamps, lonely wanderers. Puddles of sleet dark red as night fell, and then red-lit coffee shops with guitarists (of a sort),*

*bright fruit shops and souvenir and book shops: one day
we'll browse in the Strand together. Again no letter from
you today. Write to me, Caro, will you?*

New Year she spends in her flat waiting for him to ring
but he never does. She tints her hair Granada Muscat so
that it glows unexpectedly with a crimson burnish and
shocks her when she meets it in plate glass windows. She
has dinner with old friends, drinks too much and talks
too much about him. She apologizes too much, and they
say not to be silly, what on earth are friends for?

'What I like about skating,' she assures her friends, 'is
that I'm really getting somewhere, I'm making progress.
I'm not just waiting for the time to pass. I'm getting
results. I'm growing, I'm improving. Aren't I? It's visible
progress.' Giggling, she waves her brandy balloon. 'It's
all in the balance!' They just look, concern on their faces.

*

Caroline, who has been so sure that certain afternoons
were really unforgettable, finds they have gone. Like a
film only intermittently in focus, all the rest a mist. In
dreams she relives moments and wakes burning and
overjoyed. The dreams fade quickly. If he's forgetting
too, she thinks in a panic, what is there left?

She looks at the five photographs, all that she has of
him. Whenever she thinks of him now his face is in one or
other of the five expressions. Is she forgetting what he
looks like? When she sees him again, will she find herself
trying to match his face to the photographs? She goes
over old conversations. They are being eroded, and the
expressions don't fit them at all. If only I'd written them
down, she thinks.

She writes in her diary: WRITE THINGS DOWN. She
finds scribbled lines:

*Look in my face; my name is Might-have-been;
I am also called No-more, Too-late, Farewell . . .*

D.G. *Rossetti.*

She goes out in the simmering streets and sees him on

this corner or the next. He's back and he hasn't told her. It's always – well, of *course* it is! – someone else. She goes to the rink most days. Cats doze on verandahs, on a sprouting old settee left out as garbage, on brick walls. A tortoiseshell cat and a snail-coloured tabby cat, coiled and humped and with ears like horns, follow her then vanish. One day she finds a caterpillar with sparse long black fur and a hump, arching hurriedly on a wall. It looks like a tiny moulting kitten. Days later there it is again, yards further on. She is absurdly pleased. The next day it is deep under grey layers of a spider web. So what was she expecting? Immortality? Brown broken glass glows. Vomit lies on the hot footpath in clots.

She writes to him about all this and hopes he will understand. She tells him she is thinking of getting a cat: for company, she adds. So he'll know she's alone. She tells him she loves him.

She imagines that he is walking towards her. He stops to talk, seeing that she has seen him. With a smile more like a wince, out of pure courtesy he tries to chat. His shirt is open at the neck. She could lean forward and touch her lips to the hairs of his chest, except that he doesn't want her to. She remembers on a beach the hairs of his belly and groin all sunlit. Shadows of a dark tree broke over him.

'I must go, sweet,' he would say as soon as he could. 'We'll have a lunch one day, will we?'

*

One night, five weeks now since he left, the phone is suddenly ringing. His voice is heavy, blurred, and she is vague from sleep. The operator tells her to wait while he drops quarters in a coin phone. 'Darling, I can't stand it any longer,' his stifled voice is saying. 'I'm going to have to tell her. It can't go on like this. She can tell there's something wrong. I can't go on saying there's nothing *wrong* day in day out –'

'Oh, but listen. Wait!' Is he as drunk as he sounds?

'We'll get a flat,' he said. 'Look for a flat. She can have

the house. Don't tell me you've changed your mind now?'

'*No*. Let's not be rash. Let's wait till you get back and we can talk about it. We never *have*. We need time – '

' "Time will say nothing," how does it go again?'

'Oh darling.'

'Don't want me now. I see.'

'I *do*. You know I do.'

'Your three minutes are up,' the operator says. 'Are you extending your call, sir?'

Caroline persuades him to ring her again right away, reversing the charges. 'Lady ain't tired a me yet, you hear her?' he drawls to the new operator, who sniffs. He is determined, truculent, heavily offended that she is raising objections now. They ring off, both promising a letter that will explain everything. 'My mind's made up,' he insists. 'I'm going ahead and telling her tonight.'

Caroline lies awake. His too-eager eyes urge her and on their brown surface she doesn't recognize herself. Justify this, they are saying. Justify me, seduce me, adore me. Be what I dream. Am I having to pay a great price all for nothing? Her heart thudding, she lies rigid all night.

That day she rings her mother, who is both pleased and horrified. She tells the friends she had dinner with and looks up Flats To Let in the newspaper. She waits for his letter, but none comes. She tries to write to him and can't. She skates, walks in the hot streets, swims when the bay is clean. No more phone calls wake her.

*

A week later there is a letter from New York: a funny recycled New Year card mailed weeks ago. He writes of having gone to Mass on Christmas Eve at St Patrick's. Long before you reach it, he says, you can see reflections of a white spire . . . And she sees it jagged, a white spire curling and melting, swooning in glass. In a marble nave he gracefully genuflects as if in a dance. She, raised a Protestant, has never learnt to genuflect, or to dance for that matter. Her movements are not fluid but tight and graceless as a chilled swimmer's.

Wine is a help, she thinks. Wine does help, it warms and frees me. Remember to drink wine before he comes, she writes in her diary, and be bold and wild, sinuous! With the help of Chianti she answers his letter from the past. Her memory is starting to jam on times when things went wrong between them. This is fatal, she tells herself. At the moment of doubt the skater falls.

> *Darling,*
>
> *When your letter came, your New Year card, I went to the little church at the end of my street. I bought guava jelly at the stall they were holding, and went through an archway with a cool tree and lilies. From outside, the windows are embroideries of iron on glass; from inside, saints in robes of flame on their deep sky. The stone is draped like vines in Tuscany. How I wish it could bud in spring and be warmly hung with golden leaves and grapes in autumn, like the mast of Dionysos's ship — holding out its fruit in the darkness . . .*
>
> *Tell me, do the skyscrapers* (but did the hotels is what she meant) *sway in a high wind? And is there skating in summer at the Rockefeller Centre? I can skate now. I haven't fallen yet. I won't, I refuse to. I'll show you!*

It's probably too late for her letter to reach him before he leaves New York, but she mails it anyway, backdating it to before his phone call. Then she sits eating guava jelly with a spoon, regretting the letter. It reads like an essay. What has its voice to do with her voice on the phone or with his? Is there any point at which their lives touch now?

> *Will we be happy living together* (she writes in her diary)*? The only time he could stay all night wasn't a success. We were nervous and drank too much. I felt his disappointment, though he hid it courteously, without knowing what I'd done. Two days later he told me. 'You're such a selfish lover,' he added.*
>
> *'But of course I care if you're not satisfied!' I protested.*

'You mean you faked?'

'Well, I had to. You were so damn happy.'

'I spent $300 on new bedcovers for one night, does that look like I didn't care?'

Again that gasp of impatience, his hand in that gesture of despair or anger: okay, let's just forget it. On the night I just lay there in an anguish of propitiation. I thought he was feeling guilty. He left earlier in the morning than he needed to. Yet we got over this. We were overcoming our misunderstandings. Surely we'll come through?

Don't tell me he's having religious scruples now. I don't believe this!

One hot afternoon the phone rings and she grabs it wildly, but it's her mother full of news about a neighbour's grassfire turned back just in time, a dog lost and found lame. A rooster crows on the farm, miles away, glossy and smug under gumtrees heavy with dust. Sheep are grizzling on all the dry hills. To splash on horseback, she thinks, through shadows at the amber creek.

'Caroline. Is he back yet?'

'No. Well, I don't know.'

'You haven't heard at all? The bastard. He hasn't rung you?'

'He will soon, I expect.'

'Well, come up to the farm, why don't you. Come and pick apples. What's the use of languishing alone?' She laughs. 'Sorry. Mother hen. Anyway, you know. Always welcome and all that.'

'I will come up. Yes, I will. But not yet. Who have you got lined up for me now?'

She puts the phone down before her mother can think up a denial. Checkmate. Her mother will be smiling now by the west windows, the phone still in her hand. Smiling herself, Caroline takes *Couples*, a towel and a bag of nectarines and lies on the hot sand, and swims, and dries off in the late red sun.

*

A postcard then – the Lincoln Center by night – but all it says is that he's coming back on schedule, two days from the day she gets it. He can't say what flight. She is elated at first and then succumbs to a frenzied panic. What does that mean: *can't say what flight*? She doesn't, of course, dare go to the airport on the day. She waits at home. He doesn't come or ring. Speechless with dread she drags through the night and the next day. At five he knocks: he hasn't a key to this flat. They embrace, but tentatively. He is certainly himself and she has not been forgetting him at all. He exclaims how brown she is and how much thinner. He has brought cuttings, book reviews for her to read. She pours what's left of the Chianti that has got her through these last two days into glasses full of ice cubes. The ice glows red round the glittering splinters of its tiny bubbles. The glasses mist over. She tries to read while he sips and smokes and listens to a new record she has bought for the occasion, the New World Symphony. Then he gets up to go. She gazes at him.

'I can't stay, darling.' He is discomforted rather than apologetic. 'It's this welcome-back party we're going to. God, I'm a zombie from jetlag. Don't look like that. I'll stay longer some other time.'

'But we haven't talked.'

'Darling, some other time.'

She nods and tries to smile, jiggling her red ice. 'What you said on the phone? Can't you tell me what's happened?'

'Nothing's *happened*.'

'It *has*. You don't love me now.'

'Sweet, that's *not* true.'

'*Please*?'

He sits down sighing. 'I don't know. I was sure I did. I even told her so, for God's sake, once when I was blind drunk. Oh, you know, I rang you. We went through hell for days after that, all over Manhattan. But we came through. You know, I think we're closer now than we've ever been. Hell, Caro, you don't want to listen to this.

Sorry. Was it a good summer, sweet? Tell me about you.'

'I got by. It wasn't waited. *Wasted*. I learned to skate. Wait till you see Caro on ice!' But he is shaking his head. 'Let me guess: the deal is you give me up?'

He nods. 'A clean break.'

'Oh, right. Keep it clean. What did you tell her about me?'

'Not much. What could I? We don't talk about it any more. Though she did ask today –'

'Does she know you're here now?'

'No. She did ask today if I had any regrets about – you know. "Breaking with Caroline." I said no. No regrets.'

'Not a bad curtain line. Delivered with more conviction.'

'I meant it, Caro.'

'At the time.'

He looks at the time. 'God, *look* at the time,' he says, and stands up. 'It was fun, though, wasn't it? Caro, you were great.' A light kiss, and he is gone.

She drinks her wine, pulls thick woollens and gloves on, then wanders out on to the sunny Esplanade. Palms stoop and swish, sails shake on the foam of the bay. Leaves, torn off the trees, rise and sink about her as if in a fire. Summer is as good as over. And no bones broken either. Already Caro can see herself glide, a long blue shape on the ice among the other skaters, flaring through the sun's path with dust and mist and veils of snowy breath behind her; dazzled, transfigured, she turns and glides.

INHERITANCE

Here I sit in your armchair shrouded in shadows of grey
lace; my glass of red wine glows on the sill; the garden is
starlit beyond the mirroring pane.

Again and again you were taken to the hospital and
came back determined not to die. My father each time
grey with terror that you soon must. Your mind, half-
dead since your stroke, stumbled on among twisted
words and phrases, hostilities, old affections, shards of
memory. Some querulous love left for your garden and
for my little girl, Claire, whom you kept calling Paula.
Splutters of anger or distress when anything was out of
place or time. My father in his closed room tinkered with
clocks and radios, played scraps of Bach on his piano,
studied the stars by telescope. He died years ago and is
charred bones now.

Up at the hospital they said that this time you would
die. You'd given up. Why?

You used to ask me to promise not to look at your dead
body. 'That's not how I want you to remember me,
Paula,' you said. You didn't look at your own mother,
who died young. 'What remains is only the husk,' you
said, 'the soul being ascended unto the Father.' We went
with Auntie May one cold afternoon to put lilies on your
mother's grave, cold white folded lilies. I crept among
the staring statues in bony drapery. The cypress trees had
seeds like snails on their black fronds.

'Promise you'll have me cremated,' you said.

*

The first time you didn't want me to know that something serious was wrong. I was in the middle of examinations at university and must not be put off my stride. But Auntie May rang me in college.

'Paula, if they won't tell you the truth I will,' she shouted. 'It's *cancer*. Your mother might die under the knife. *Yes*. You ask your father.'

Cancer was what I had always most feared for you. You smoked such a lot. You rolled your own. Godgies, I called them. (You loved my baby talk.) Pipes and lipsticks and lollipops were all godgies, and the little stalks that boys could pee through, but not my father's bicycle pump which was the hogfig. Daddy hated your godgies too. You lit the first, convulsed with deep coughs, at daybreak. I delayed opening my bedroom door and letting in the smoky breath of the rest of the house. In winter on the way to school – streetlamps still gold, a grey light spreading – I watched in disgust as white smoke poured out of me.

In the holidays when we went to the city for lunch and a show I wouldn't sit in a smoking compartment and flounced on my own to a non-smoker. Perched on a green seat by a shuddering double window I watched bridges and factories trundle beyond my dusty shadow. On the city platform you were waiting, breathing smoke through an angry smile.

At ten, on some dull visit, leafing by lamplight through old magazines while you grown-ups played cards, I read that cigarettes caused lung cancer. I tore the page out. 'Oh, what rubbish,' you said. Tearful and urgent, waiting on the corner that frosty night for a brown bus home: 'Mummy,' I whimpered. 'Please, please stop. You'll get cancer and die. Daddy, you tell her.'

'It's your mother's own business, Paula. Just keep quiet.'

You never got lung cancer. Eight years ago after your stroke the doctors made you stop smoking. My father and I weren't mean. We kept quiet.

*

When I rang from college, my father denied that it was cancer you had.

'You know what your Auntie May's like, lovey. Always got the wind up about something,' he soothed. 'Mum's got to go in for a minor op., that's all. A fissure of the anus. Now you do your best. We're proud of our girl.'

But it was cancer of the bowel. You survived the colostomy and learned to fasten plastic bags to the new hole cut in your belly. You've had to do it for nearly twenty years. You were both cool after that with Auntie May, for having interfered. But my results weren't bad.

By then I was deep in first love and that was all that mattered. He was married. I never told you. He behaved like a gentleman and paid for the abortion. In all that summer of muggy heat and secrecy I only wrote you a letter or two. I'm sorry.

When that was over I hitchhiked down to see you in your bedroom that Dad had moved out of by then. In the hot noon darkness crowded with old furniture you lay asleep, tangled in bedclothes, your lamp still on. Your mouth gulped, grimaced, when I stepped inside.

'Hullo, Mum.'

'Paula! Is that you?'

Tears, glowing, trickled down your furrowed throat.

'Are you all right, Mum?'

'Paula!' Your voice blurring in the pillow. 'Why didn't you ever come?'

Later, after your shower, you called me into the bathroom to show me by its furred yellow light. I had never seen you naked. You hesitated, frail and shaking, your knees slack; then took the towel away. Your eyes rolled up in appeal. From hip to hip your belly grinned at me with crooked lips. On one side, your new anus, a puckered bud, a hole. Your nipples lolled, pink eyeballs staring down. Under the belly's sag nestled the shaggy grey chin of your groin.

'Is it still sore?'

'Not too bad.'

'It doesn't look too bad.'

You smiled at last, and I kissed you. Your wet suede cheek.

*

At Claire's age, at seven or so, I remember reproaching you for looking so flabby, wrinkled and sick. Why don't you look pretty like other mothers? I persisted. You were close on fifty, no longer pretty, but loved. The grocer sold you more butter, the butcher more meat, than you ever had coupons; old ladies poking in their dry flower beds straightened stiff backs and held you up with gossip; neighbours were in and out all day for coffee. The tram conductors on our way to the second-hand bookstore told you their life stories. One whole summer in the hot twilight before bedtime you read me and my playmates *Alice in Wonderland* from my faded green copy that smelled, still smells, of autumn leaves.

Daddy read me music in bed. Scales, crotchets and quavers. FACE and Every Good Boy Deserves Food. We hummed the first bars of sonatas he was going to teach me. But I had no ear, and disappointed him.

Waking in terror of cages and shadows and furtive rustlings I would call out to you. It was always he who came, he the lighter sleeper. 'Mu-um, my leg's got cramps.' His knee joints crackling at every step down the dark passage. He would switch on my dazing light and sit rubbing my calves, wryly yawning.

'Not better yet?' he would sigh.

'No. Daddy, can I come into your bed?'

'No, lovey. Back to sleep now.'

'But I'll dream about the hospital!'

'No, you won't.'

'Will you leave the light on?'

'All right. The passage light. Night night, Snooks.'

He would kiss my cheek and stalk crackling back to the dark room you two slept in. Snoring in counterpoint.

*

I was always dreaming about the hospital. This great terror of hospitals, all my life. At five I spent six weeks in one with scarlet fever. You dressed me in my best brown jumper and skirt and Daddy took me there in a taxi. A nurse bathed me in phenol. The children's ward was long, cold, dim. Its balcony had a high wire fence that I clambered up one day for a dare. I was caught, punished with isolation; the nurse had short red hair and an angry contempt that stunned me. You rang the matron daily. No visitors were allowed for fear of infection. The fenced ward was our prison. Often I overshot the bedpan and rubbed the sheet for hours after, to dry it; the white cage of my bed jiggling, tinkling. I could see one skylight with stars behind it turn blue, grey, gold each morning. Nurses sponged us and replaited our plaits tightly. When Daddy came for me at last, I refused to speak. My brown jumper and skirt were brought out folded. I had given up hope of ever seeing them or home again. It was a sunny day. A stiff wind blowing.

*

As he aged and in retirement became remote – brittle, silent – his nights were more disturbed and the crackling of his joints woke me several times a night as he crept outside, but by then I never called.

My knee joints crackle too. I take after him. Daddy's girl. We were skinny, to your plump. Daddy's little skinnamalink. He dinked me on the bar of his bicycle to vacant lots where in other summers circuses had appeared overnight, soiled elephants shambled; to clamber through the golden skeletons of the new houses. He lifted me high into our gumtree to pick off its crouched caterpillars. He built bonfires like haystacks and lit Catherine wheels warily. He held my cheeks in rough palms to guide my gaze at galaxies and constellations. Our trees waved giant hushed shadows over skyfuls of stars.

You weigh five stone now.

On that last day, when you trotted in right on time with his morning tea, he lay flung half-off the bed in an attitude of terror, his grey eyes wide; heart pills all over the sunny floorboards. I was two hours getting here. An aged, sorrowful child, you sat numbly for hours by the window; scurried to pack away his clothes; on the telephone mumbled over and over broken self-reproaches, despair. You had squabbled over breakfast. He had trudged back to bed in a sulk. Feeling sick, he said.

'Mum, you couldn't have known.'

'Should have. Should. Oh yes. Oh.'

*

Once his clothes were packed off to the Brotherhood, the piano and telescope sold, you asked me to find you a flat near ours in the city. I looked around on my days off: it had to be a ground-floor flat because of your heart. There was nothing suitable. After a couple of months you said you'd changed your mind, you weren't helpless, thanks all the same. You'd stay put.

I wish I was one of those women who give up their lives to care for the old and sick.

You always hoped I'd want to be a nurse when I grew up. When I got out of hospital you had made me a nurse costume. When I was twelve you talked me into spending Saturday afternoons helping at the hospital with friends from school. The patients were old, paralysed, incontinent, blind, abandoned. We folded linen and peeled potatoes. We hacked off the green shells of pumpkins, polished and grooved, with orange seeds and rags of flesh hanging in their wombs. One afternoon the nurses asked me to feed a young blind man his custard. It was a privilege: nicknamed Freddie, he was their favourite. In my awkwardness I let hot custard trickle down Freddie's neck and puddle in his pillow as he lay smiling up. Tears spilled from his white eyes. Frantic, I mopped his raspy throat and chin, I was too ashamed to ever go back. He kept asking after me, my friends reported. 'Oh;

Paula,' you said. Shaking your grey head. 'You are heartless.'

*

We were down here just last Sunday. Whimpering, you bared your sore, swollen ankles. 'Oh don't want. Turn into a vegetable.' Your veined eyes round as you faltered, saying that. You spent most of the day in bed and refused to eat. On Tuesday the Meals on Wheels man found you lying on the kitchen floor and called the ambulance. The matron rang me at work.

'Can you come down? Doctor says her heart's grossly enlarged. She's very weak.'

'She'll be all right, though, won't she?'

'Well, we can't say. Come down if possible. She's asked for you.'

You'd asked for me.

I took time off and drove down with Claire to the little bush hospital. A day of midwinter spring, with the lamps lit all afternoon along the shore. Kookaburras and magpies in the shabby gumtrees in the grounds. From your window, late sun glazing the hollow sea. Woodsmoke from chimneys in the hills towered.

When you had your stroke a few days before Claire was born, we had been estranged for months: my child would have no father. I lumbered in to visit you in the city hospital, kissed your cheek and flopped gasping in a chair with my offering of daffodils. You could hardly move. Slowly your stiff mouth drooled words.

'What, Mum?'

'You. Go. Now.'

'What did you say?'

'Want. You. Go. Now.'

I flung the gaudy flowers down and went.

*

Last Sunday Claire found some of your old photographs. She brought one in to show us, the one of you and Auntie May smiling on a staircase. Two little sepia girls with frilly dresses and bows in their hair.

'Have you still got that dress, Mummy? Please can I have it?'

'No, that was Granma's dress.'

'But you've got it on!'

'No, that's not me. That's Granma. When she was your age.'

'Oh. Have you still got it, Granma?'

You smiled, shaking your head. That was all. Later I found the photo in the rubbish bin. I took it out, stained and creased, when you weren't looking.

A while ago I played all the tapes that Dad had made, mostly of broadcasts of organ recitals. His beloved fugues wheezed, thumped and groaned. In the middle of a slow passage I heard him sigh. I played it again. There it was. His deep sigh, embedded in the music.

I told you about it. Would you like to hear it? I'd play it for you. You shook your shaggy head. Were your eyes blank, or hostile? You would have loved to hear his voice, wouldn't you? You would have.

You turned your head away.

*

This time I brought red tulips propped in a carafe on the locker like five sunlit glasses of red wine. They are opening unseen beside you now, showing their yellow throats. Inside each are six rods of black velvet like the legs of an upturned insect; and a three-pronged tongue, its colour lost in the glow.

Your mottled hand crawled to huddle in mine, a dry claw for all these years plump again now with the same fluid that was welling in your ankles. In your lungs.

'Sorry dear. Accident. Shower.'

'You fell in the shower?'

'No, no.' Shaking your angry matted head. 'Accident. Bowel. Mess in bathtub.'

'Oh, Mum, that's nothing! I'll clean it up!'

'Disgusted.'

'Of course not. You couldn't help it. Don't be silly!'
You rolled your filmed eyes up to gaze at me.
'Thank you. For coming.'
'I'll be back tonight. Now you get some sleep.'
I kissed your hollow cheek. Your cropped grey hair sodden, fetid, all on end. You nodded and twisted to watch me go back to Claire, anxiously on tiptoe in the doorway. We waved to your mute face watching. Watching us go.

I dropped Claire at the Smiths' to play and came back alone to sit here drinking as night fell. The wine was dark as blood by lamplight. Remembering.

I drove back alone in visiting hours. I was too late. Your body, wracked as if in childbirth, was heaving up off the bed with every gasp; your mouth a mute howl; your eyes bulging, blood-stained. I called you. Nothing. No hope now, the doctor said. Did you know I was there? When I was holding your swollen hand, could you feel my hand? You'd asked for me. Did you want me to go now? I'd always promised not to look. I crept away.

What should I have done?

I picked Claire up. Fast asleep by their fire, she hardly stirred when I carried her to the car and then to bed. 'Read me *Alice*,' she mumbled, but fell asleep again.

I sat up gulping wine. Your wracked grimace accused me. So weak, how had you found such strength, such anguish, to fight for each breath, each heartbeat, one by one? I sat slobbering with shame and dread until the telephone rang and the doctor murmured that my mother had passed away, and suggested an undertaker. So it was over, you had cast your loose old skin: it lay there stiffening in warm sheets. Nurses will sponge you now and stop up all your openings – the warped anus, too, in your seamed belly. You used to apologize to new nurses for it. At home you flinched as wind purred out, escaping the taut bag; with strained composure visitors would ignore the sudden smell.

Stars roof your luminous garden. The trees are still. Empty snail shells, small brown skulls, litter the flower

beds and the frosty grass. A blue glow covers the fuchsia
with its dangling bells, the japonica's red paper petals, the
studded daphne. Pale lilies are coiled around their dusty
rods. Soon your dry wisteria vine will hang out its frilled
mauve pods in bunches.

In one of the grey snapshots by the bedlamp in your
room you and Dad walk elated hand in hand past the
pillars and steps of the GPO, just married at forty at the
start of the War. In the other you grin squinting into the
sun on the verandah, your only baby, bald and glum,
cuddled in tentative white-downed arms. My lifetime
ago.

*

The shower taps are smudged with brown. You told
me. The soap as well. Splatters here and there blotch the
grey enamel of the tub. With rubber gloves on I scrub
away the hard brown spots, pour boiling water over and
wrap gloves, soap and steel wool in newspaper before I
ram them in the bin.

Stooped here in splashing yellow water, sludge oozing
from your hole and between the puffed fingers that tried
to hold it back, did you decide to die?

Rust is tarnishing the steam-furred mirror. I am shiny
under the dusty globe, my lips black from the wine. The
dim skin of my eyes is bruised, wilted. My bones are
yellow ridges. Hollows lie dark along my jaw and throat.

Claire's tread thumps down the passage. In the mirror
her sleepy face that was mine once. Her warm hair all on
end.

'Granma just died, darling one,' I say.

'Won't we ever see her again?'

'No. She wouldn't like us to.'

'Does she look horrible?'

I shake my head. She leans frowning in the doorway:

'This is our house now, isn't it?'

'Yes.'

'Are we coming to live down here?'

'Maybe in summer.'
'Where's Granma's soul now?'
'I don't know.'
'Not here!' she shrieks.
'No. Not here.'
'With Granpa's?'
'Nobody knows.'
'Can I come into your bed? And leave the light on?'
'All right. The passage light.'
She comes and presses her hot face against me.
'Mummy,' she whimpers.

THE CAPTAIN'S HOUSE

Home, in the five years that Barbara had been married to
Andoni Dimitriou, had been one rented house or flat
after another. This summer, for two months, home was
the Captain's house, as everyone called it, in a fishing
town in Halkidiki not far from Mount Athos.

A two-storey villa in a back street fenced with dusty
oleanders, it glowed white in the summer sun and moved
its shadow like a cape around it on the rough earth. Spare
and shabby, the house of a plain fisherman who owned
the town's sole fishing *kaïki*, it had rooms washed in sea
colours of white, green, grey, blue. In the upstairs rooms
all five Dimitrious slept: the baby in with Andoni and
Barbara; three-year-old Vassilaki with his grandmother,
whom Barbara called Mama and thought of as Andoni's
Mother. These rooms all had splintered shutters that had
warped and floors of grey planks which formed the ceiling of the one long room below. From downstairs, when
the lights went on upstairs, each plank glowed, rimmed
with gold. It was like looking up from the shallow water
under a jetty. In all the ground-floor windows – their
ledges painted dark green and so deep-set that Barbara
soon took to sitting there and reading in the afternoon
when the household slept – branches of oleander and
hazelnut made even the light green.

'Always reading, Varvaro *mou*,' Andoni's mother
chided her.

'I hardly ever get the chance,' said Barbara in her
careful Greek. 'I never would, without you here to help
me.' Which was true. 'Besides, I keep falling asleep.'

Andoni's mother smiled. 'Always Australian books.

You should at least read Greek books.'

'Mama, I do. More Greek books than Andoni.'

'Well, Andoni doesn't need to.'

Andoni's mother did more than help, she ran the house. There was no refrigerator, so Andoni's mother borrowed from the Kapetanissa, their landlady, three wire cages to hang from the ceiling to keep food cool and safe. She found a neighbour with a Maltese cow to sell them milk for Vassilaki. She sent Andoni to buy fish alive, and at a discount, from the Kapetanios, when the boats came in at daybreak on wave after wave of faint water. All the melons, tomatoes and cucumbers and peppers, yellow peaches and grapes that the family could want were sold door to door by yelling hawkers with donkey carts and brass-panned scales: no one could haggle like Andoni's mother. She befriended the Kapetanissa, who was in and out all day with a new-laid egg for Vassilaki, a handful of figs, a cup of gritty honey. They even went to church together.

Voula, the Kapetanissa's unmarried daughter, took to the Dimitrious no less eagerly.

'Anyone would think Voula had no home to go to,' Andoni's mother muttered to Barbara as they made lunch.

'Are you tired of her?' Voula's squeals and trills of laughter rang out upstairs, where she was romping with Vassilaki. 'Vassilaki adores her, though.'

'Well. She is a teacher.'

Not that that explained it. How many such sumptuous honey-skinned girls would waste their time on a small boy?

'I suppose she must love children. And she can practise her English on us.' Because Barbara spoke English to Vassilaki, to Andoni's mother's secret annoyance.

'You think that? And you're not jealous? More fool you, then.'

'Why? I want him to be happy.'

'Who, Varvara?'

'Vassilaki. Who else?'

'One way to a man's heart, for what that's worth,' said Andoni's mother drily, 'is through his children.'

'Is it? When I am not so tired,' said Barbara no less drily, 'I must try it.' She chopped an onion savagely.

Andoni's mother shrugged. Typically, Varvara had missed the point. What use were warnings? No, Varvara was so tired!

So when Andoni's brother and his wife burst into the Captain's house during lunch, insisting that they were taking everyone – everyone, yes, Voula too – for a drive to Ouranoupoli in that bright new Fiat parked outside: and Barbara said no, she was so tired . . .

'You *go!*' Andoni's mother snapped. '*Ma*, what's wrong with the woman? So *tired!*'

Everyone gaped.

'*Aptokinito*,' gloated Vassilaki. 'Mama, *aptokinito*.' He loved cars.

'*Affftokinito*,' said Barbara automatically.

Andoni's mother glared. 'With Voula, eight,' she said. 'Eight in one car. Ridiculous. And the car is too hot for the baby, remember the bus trip here? I am more tired,' she told Barbara. 'I will stay and mind the baby.'

'But, Mama! What about his feeds?'

'I can find a bottle. He can have cow's milk. Once won't hurt him. Varvara, did I raise six of my own to manhood, or did I not?'

'Please, I'd rather stay home.' They had planned to bottle figs that afternoon, she and Andoni's mother and the Kapetanissa.

It was no use arguing. Barbara went: wedged in the back between her sister-in-law and Voula, with Vassilaki on her lap; the brothers sat arguing in the front about Greece and NATO.

*

They had intended to go no further than Ouranoupoli. It had a bay with boats, shops and *tavernes*, and a medi-aeval tower, gaunt and unsteady, where an Australian woman was said to live: swallows swooped shrilling up and down its walls. But the town beach turned out to be stony and the water turbid green, so they drove on to the end of the road, the border of Mount Athos. Athos, the Holy Mountain, had a border with fences and gates, and a hut with a low wall for the guard. Signs in foreign languages forbade females and wheeled vehicles to enter. Andoni's brother parked here, under pine trees simmering with sun and cicadas. Beyond glittered the sea and a beach of fine white sand like salt, where the only shade was a twisted pinnacle of grey rock here and there, some knee deep in sand, others in water. Barbara hurried Vassilaki to the shelter of the biggest rock to change. Everyone else, tugging bathers on, flinging clothes off, hopping on scorched feet, went thundering straight in with a yell.

'At last,' sighed Barbara, lying in the shallows among the standing rocks with Vassilaki.

The water was so warm, so nearly invisible, it was as if they two were afloat in air. To every hair on their bodies bright bubbles clung, magnified.

A catamaran had anchored just offshore.

'Look at that!' Andoni's brother spat water out. 'Foreigners. All over our best beaches.'

'More foreigners?' called Barbara.

'Not you, Varvara. We brought you.'

Two white heads on brown bodies clambered up on to the catamaran, bronze buttocks glistening.

'Wonderful,' snarled Andoni's brother. 'Germans, I bet. Or Swedes.' The catamaran was souring his joy in his ruby Fiat.

'Who cares?' shouted Andoni. 'Where's the ball?'

'Here!' Voula threw it. 'Catch!'

They plunged deeper. 'Come on, Vassilaki,' called Andoni. 'Come and play ball!'

'Nao! Nao!' he yelled in frantic English.

'Ach, Andoni,' Barbara reproached him.

' "Ach, Andoni," ' whined Andoni. 'Why can't he swim?'

'He's only little.'

'Your face is all red. You're burning.'

'Already?' Barbara's white skin would only ever burn and freckle and peel; no suncream could stop it. Vassilaki burned easily too. 'How much?' But he shrugged, swimming off to the others.

She towed Vassilaki by his hands to the beach: being a boat was a good game. A promise of sandcastles and he let her carry him to the short shadow of their rock. She dragged her dress on, stiff with dry milk. 'Boo!' Down came his oiled shirt over his straw head. 'Now. Sandcastles.'

But: 'Vassila-ki! Vassilaki, *balla*!' echoed across the water. And Andoni was thrashing and wallowing, waving his copper arms at him, tossing the ball. 'Vassilaki!'

'Why I can't swim?' wailed Vassilaki. 'Why, Mama?'

'We'll go back in soon,' she said.

'Now I want.'

'First let's make a sandcastle. One like this rock.'

'H-how?'

'Watch.'

Crouching at the water line she packed wet sand into a mound first, then squeezed soggy handfuls over it, trickling the sand down like candlewax until there it was: a twisted pinnacle. Vassilaki dug out more wet sand. Joyfully they made another one.

'Look!' He waded in knee deep to call the others. 'Come and see what I made!'

'*Bravo, bravo,*' called his father.

Voula splashed out. 'What a clever darling!' She swooped to kiss him.

'Yes.' He was shyly proud.

'Is one for me?'

'They mine,' he said doubtfully. 'Mine and Mama's.'

'Then I'm going.' Laughing, she ran back in.

'You make some too!' Vassilaki wailed after her. 'Voula *mou*! Voula *mou*.'

'When she comes back.' Barbara hugged him. 'Let's go and sleep under a tree.'

'I thirsty.'

'Come on, then.'

She carried him on her back up the hot sand to the pine trees where the car stood glowing. There was still some water in a bottle glittering on the front seat. He drank, and made a face. She drank too. Then he licked the last hot drops. 'Who that man?' he said.

On the holy side of the border wall a little man in black was fussing about, pulling up a bucket from the well, clicking to his dusty hens, chopping a blood-red watermelon open. Vassilaki trotted over, but the man had gone into the hut. Yawning, Barbara took a woven *kilimi* from the car and spread it on the pine needles.

'Madame!' The man was calling her. '*E*, Madame!'

You fanatical old prude, Barbara thought. But no: he was beckoning her. And as she faltered, he grinned and hoisted two fat slices of watermelon up, one in each withered hand.

'*Karpouzi!*' gloated Vassilaki.

The guard brightened. Never mind their pale hair and sunburn, they were not complete foreigners.

'*Efharisto.*' Barbara bowed, accepting the slices. A bench had been built into the wall on both sides, like a stile: the guard sat there and motioned to them to sit opposite. Vassilaki huddled close, gazing. 'What do you say?' she prompted.

'*Paristo.*' The guard looked as pleased as if he had got it right. Boldly Vassilaki sank his face into the melon. 'Can we see in your house?' he mumbled.

'Sssh, no,' Barbara said. 'Mama can't.'

'Oh. *Why?*'

'The Panagia said,' smiled the guard. 'The Mother of God. The Holy Mountain is Hers, it is Her garden. No other females can come here.'

Hens can, Barbara thought. Aloud she said, 'I've never believed all that.' The guard blinked. She ploughed on in her stilted Greek. 'Can it be true that the Panagia is jealous and hates other females? What if She wanted the Holy Mountain for females only? But the Church changed it round?'

'Ha ha!' But he was ruffled. 'You tourists. You're all Catholics and Reds and Anarchists. Why don't you stay home? Antichrists!'

'I live in Greece.'

'Since when, Madame? If I may ask?'

'Six years.'

'*Po po.* Only? You have too much to learn, Madame. May the Panagia grant you enlightenment.'

Every bite of the melon uncovered seeds sown like stones in snow, thawing red snow. She flicked them out with a finger and bit deep. The guard spat his seeds through a gap in his furred teeth straight at the Fiat: pfoo pfoo. Vassilaki stared; then he tried it. Barbara laughed. At once the guard relented.

'If I may ask.' He gave a dry cackle. 'You come from Italy?'

'No. Greece.' She pointed. 'See. Greek plates.'

'Before six years?'

'Ah yes. Australia.'

'*Ma! Afstraleea!*' As if that explained it. 'Why do you live so far from home?'

'Home is here now.' Home, now, was the Captain's house. 'My husband is Greek. And our boys. Life is beautiful here.' She stood up. Her head was thumping. 'Well, time for sleep,' she announced.

'Nao! Pfoo!'

'*Po po,*' frowned the guard. 'Is that how good boys speak to their Mamas? Wash him down first, Mama,' he said in much the same tone. Red juice was drying on Vassilaki's throat and arms. 'Do you want the bees to eat him? Wait.'

He took the green rinds away and brought a jug of well water. She sluiced Vassilaki down, and then herself. The water made tracks in their coating of salt and sand. With a sigh she settled down with her arms round Vassilaki on the hairy stripes of the *kilimi*.

'*Melissa!*' Vassilaki cried out: there was a bee, or a wasp. But it floated heavily away, vanished among the pines. 'Will the bees eat me?'

'Not now you're washed.'

'Where are the bees?'

'Asleep.'

'What do they eat?'

'Honey.'

'Mama, I still thirsty.'

'Oh, darling.'

'I want a drink.'

'There isn't anything. Well water's bad.'

'Moolk.'

'No milk. Only this milk.' She patted her taut breasts.

'That moolk for our baby.'

'He's not here.'

Vassilaki squirmed. 'Nao!' he giggled.

'Have some.' She unbuttoned her dress. 'Just suck like our baby. Don't bite me!'

'Nao!'

'All right, nao. I'm going to sleep.'

She had closed her eyes, dozed off, before she felt him fumble, then firmly close his lips on her nipple. She sighed as her milk let down. Vassilaki recoiled; milk sprayed him. She felt him rub his eyes. But she had not moved, so he came back to the hard nipple and sucked. Languidly she stretched, as if asleep, when the first breast had gone slack, to bring the other one closer. Then they must both have fallen asleep, for when she opened her eyes with a shiver the shadows were longer over them, and cooler, and Vassilaki was in her arms with his back against her. 'Wake up,' she murmured. He moaned, his eyes flickered. No one was in sight, not even the guard, but from the beach came music and voices, laughing: Andoni's hooting laugh, a descant from Voula. 'Wake up.' She nudged him again. He yawned, stretching.

'Want to swim now?'

'Yes!'

'Want to do *tsisia*?' They never called it weewee, always *tsisia*.

'Nao.'

Holding his hand she trudged down the shadow-pitted sand, past the others (there they were, dancing to disco music on the radio), past the sandcastles. The catamaran was fluttering out to sea. '*Addio, varka*,' Vassilaki told it sorrowfully. '*Paei*, Mama. *Pou paei?*'

'A long way away.'

'*Spiti paei?*'

'Yes. It's going home. Come on.' They surged loudly in, gasping as the cold clutched them. The others called, waved, then chased them in with shrieks and swam into deeper water. Long furrows and flurries followed them. In the low sun the shallows were as warm and golden as creek water.

'Mama, *tsisia*.'

'Oh. You said no.'

'*Tsisia!*' And the water clouded for a moment about his plump legs. He blushed; his mouth crumpled.

'Darling. It doesn't matter.'

'*Tsisia* in the water?'

'You couldn't help it. It was the watermelon.'

'Why?'

'Just kick it away,' she said. 'No one will know.' Relieved, he kicked and pounded and splashed. It was too much: wading further away, she let her own *tsisia* flow warm between her thighs and dim the water. Airily she backstroked to where Vassilaki was.

'Ooh! Mama!'

'What?'

'You did *tsisia*!'

'I did not.'

'I saw you.'

'You were too far. It was sand you saw.'

Forcing a smile, she kicked up a cloud of sand in the golden water. But he pouted. He knew she was lying. 'All right, I did *tsisia*,' she said. 'Don't tell anyone.'

'I will!'

'No. Don't.'

Vassilaki's uncle and aunt were calling him from the shore: they had found a crab. Vassilaki plunged away and

Barbara made for the deep water at last. If he did tell, how scornful they would be, she thought. Andoni's dowdy placid Australian cow, bony and speckled; oozing milk in her sleep; pissing where she stood . . . She splashed in long duck-dives into darker, cooler water and surfaced out of breath alongside Voula and Andoni.

They had not seen her coming. They sprang apart straight away. But Andoni had been holding Voula's arm with such a look on his face – of tender regret, of consolation, of sympathy – that now Barbara knew.

She knew. Voula gasped, whipped her arm free with a mutter of words to Andoni, indistinct words. And Andoni smiled. 'Race you two to the beach,' he sang out, and set off with arms thrashing, half-hidden in froth.

'Ach, Varvara *mou*,' said Voula, rubbing her arm. 'A big jellyfish sting me. You coming?'

Barbara stared in silence as Voula swam in Andoni's wake to the shore, only once stopping to float, her head dipped back to let her hair stream out on the shaken tawny water. You were right, Mama, Barbara foresaw herself saying at home. But no; how could she? Andoni was wading ashore. He and Voula would go on pretending nothing had happened. Childishly, Barbara felt cheated. As if, just because they were caught, they had to stop playing! Varvara *mou*, Andoni's mother would smile: You think that?

Chilled, she struggled ashore, and flopped down on her towel in sand like warm corn meal. She squeezed her salty eyes shut. Her breasts were fat white bags again. Why had she come? What if the baby was crying? Had he taken a bottle for Andoni's mother? Maybe he wouldn't. She imagined him crying, hungry: his red crumpled little face! And Andoni's mother and the Kapetanissa in the green-gold kitchen below, much too busy boiling figs in syrup to hear him cry. If only she had stayed home! Besides, the baby never slept well in the afternoons. Then the sun burned on the upstairs walls of the Captain's house, so that its heavy light filled the rooms with golden slats and with shadows. Even with the shutters closed and the panes wide open there was no movement in the air that lay over the sweat-soaked sheets; only small flies humming in circles.

'You all right?' Andoni spoke behind her in a stifled voice; for the first time all day, in English.

'Me? Yes.' Their shadows joined, long on the sand. The sun was withering. 'It's the baby,' she said.

'My mother look after him.'

He rested his head on the curve of her shoulder: the nearest his pride would let him come to saying sorry.

'Ach, Andoni,' she sighed.

'We be home soon. Before night we be home.'

She lightly kissed his rough hair. Home, for long weeks, was the Captain's house.

WOMAN IN A MIRROR

She had a painting that Peter had given her. In it a blue-headed fish lay alive or dead on a wooden table in a stone room lit by one white-washed archway. Dark waves towered beyond it. Inside in the calm, there was a jug of wine or water beside the fish, a knife and fork, a goblet, one twisted chair, and a cold glow off the sea.

'Because you love the sea,' he had said. He had loved mountains.

'He who does not enjoy solitude will not love free-dom,' Schopenhauer wrote. She had printed that under the painting.

But must he who loves freedom enjoy solitude?

Behind her the sun beat in gold slats through the blinds. The child stirred, still asleep. He was flushed. Bubbles of sweat gleamed on him. His hair was damp. He lay naked, white and sturdy, a big boy for three, very calm, very self-contained. Peter's boy, but not like him. When he woke, they could go to the beach. It was hot for April.

She took her dress off and watched the woman in the mirror stroke oil on herself. She was long and flexible, but thin. Her breasts drooped over her ribs. How they had swelled, white with milk and netted with thick veins, while she was feeding the child. Only to shrink and hang down, little drab pouches. Silver tracks were left on them, and inside her loose thighs too, and on her belly, there in the centre where it had bulged until her navel turned inside out, quaking when the child moved inside. Like crushed velvet, David said it was. Peter had never seen it. Peter, who for years had known her perfectly;

who had not lived even to see the child born, but had died on a mountain road in Yugoslavia.

The Adriatic there was a sea stiller than any other, as still as the sky. Grey islands floated in it. A fisherman in his boat on the shingle showed them a fluted pink shell-fish that glowed like an ear in the sun, like a red candle when the wax has dripped. When Peter asked what it was, the man croaked a word, and laughed when they tried to say it. 'Let's have a swim,' she said, walking into the water and stooping to dabble her hand in it: her feet glowed, huge on the pebbles. 'Before we tackle the mountains.'

They were a white wall in the east.

'No time,' said Peter. 'We'll be lucky if the road's still open now past Titograd.'

A broad woman had come crunching down the shingle with fish, a whole bunch of brown fish hooked by their bony lips, shimmering.

'Fish! She thinks we want to buy fish!'

'Well, we don't. When would we cook it? Look, if the passes are closed, we're going to have to backtrack up the whole Dalmatian coast in any case. If not, we'll be swim-ming and eating fish in Greece tomorrow.'

The fisherman and his wife exchanged a look. The woman bent with a groan to dip her bunch of fish in the sea and swung them up high, nodding: see, fresh. Water fell flashing from them.

'It's so warm, though! So still and clear.'

'*Fish*,' said the woman suddenly. They all laughed. But Peter was impatient. Wasn't she the one who hated taking risks? So they shook hands with the couple and drove on east into the mountains.

Now she sat with her legs apart to see the fur and the red ridges it enveloped, crinkled like a small hen's comb. Hidden in the warm hollows inside was a gristly knob, her cervix, with the thread of the IUD emerging. Tomorrow all the quiet women in the stuffy waiting room at the Hospital would go in one by one and lie back with their bent knees apart. The doctors' hands in glittering rustling plastic would palp their soft red masses. Some of them would have cancer.

'Cancer of the cervix? That's impossible!' she had protested the first time. 'I'm only thirty-five! Why? Is it the IUD?'

Could death and decay be growing where the child grew, so soon after?

The doctor was patient. No, it wasn't the IUD. It probably wasn't cancer. She had had two tests now, though, and abnormal cells had been found both times. At the Women's Hospital they would do definitive tests. 'Make the appointment today,' he said. 'There'll be a long wait. These things can be left too late, you know. Don't put it off.'

'You fool,' she said to the face in the bright mirror. 'You coward. You were the sensible one. You never took risks.'

She had let months go by.

If she dared to ring David, he might be some comfort. David? she could say. It's me. Can you come over? I know, but sneak out for a little while. Please, it's important. They think I have cancer. Yes.

No. Impossible. She had never rung him. She had never even looked up his number. It was understood that she would never ring him. His wife would suspect. And she could never tell him this. He would hate to think of her diseased, doomed, monstrously invaded in there. He would never want her again. Once or twice a fortnight he came to stroke her and cling, and turn her over at the end so that she was any woman, and then bore between her thighs, barred with sunlight. She loved him a little. He was afraid she might.

She put on her blue bathers, glossy and pale as the sea. The child sighed. 'Hey, wake up,' she whispered. He was beautiful, crossly moving in his sleep his sturdy white arms and legs on the damp patch of his sweat. She kissed his cheek. 'Wake up, come on.'

I have a strong white body, she thought, still free of pain, streaked with silver and sunlight. The child, the sea,

freedom and solitude. And more time, Please.
More time.

*

On the tramline a long sheath of grey dust and twigs was trying to move. The child picked it up. A casemoth. From the little cap a blind brown and orange snake-like head nodded out. She helped the child find a ledge on the grey palm bole where it would be safe, and it groped around there, wagging heavily, the velvet neck of its case wrinkling with the strain like an elderly wrestler's.

'Will the casemoss die, Mummy?'

'No, not now.'

They wandered across to the beach. The sand was deep gold, pitted with shadow. The child paddled, naked in rings of water, looking for shells. Afloat all around him, the gulls stared. She tied up her hair and waded into the cold clear sea and swam off, splitting the yellow sky, turning and drifting. Angrily he called her back. There were deep shells to get for him. She was mirrored, stooping over the sea, a woman of glass shimmering, blurring her own image with slow drops of water. As she swam back he flung splashes at her and stumbled away laughing.

They sat on the towel and admired her shells and his. He put the best ones in her bag. She had oranges in it. She peeled one and pulled its striped segments apart. In that late light they shone, crescents striped inside like ice or quartz, and beaded: warm and very sweet, ripe autumn oranges. She split another one and they ate it.

Chilled, she changed awkwardly out of her wet bathers under her dress and the towel, then pulled on the child's shorts for him. 'The pier, Mummy': he was dragging at her hand. Now a flow of deep light was all over the sky and the drawn skin of the bay. Palms moved against it, black as rooster tails, flourished, then still. A woman with long straight grey hair sat perched beyond them, busily painting.

'My tutor always did say never to try a sunset,' she

called across cheerily, 'but how could I resist this? I'll make him eat his words!'

As the sky dimmed and a pale moon rose, she sighed and stood back. The child asked to see. The woman showed them shyly and turned to pack up. Her sky and sea were streaks of orange, vermilion, chrome yellow; the pier and the boats, all the hulls and strung masts, black; and there they were too, the child and she, drooping beside a bollard, her hair and her hands spread out.

'Who's them?'

'That's us.'

'You don't look like that, Mummy.'

'Ssh. I like it very much,' she said, smiling at the woman's smile.

The child went to make friends with a man fishing. Left alone, she watched a domed jellyfish come lolling into the green water under the pier. It was not aware of her, of boats and a pier, of the city's faint towers of light swaying over it. Were there beings just as unknowably watching her as she watched the jellyfish, with a vague detached goodwill? It would have been a comfort to believe there were.

Once she had been shown a painting in which reflected lights on a river leaped and faded in the black sky. 'The river runs through Zagreb,' the owner explained. 'The lights are dead souls. There were massacres that winter of the War. The artist fled. Corpses and chunks of ice choked the river.'

We drove through Zagreb, she thought. A grim stone city. Was there a river? She couldn't remember one.

White and orange lights were lit all around the edges of the bay.

It was near Zagreb, wasn't it, that Peter pulled up at a farm and asked a little boy to fill our water-can? There was a Jack-and-Jill well in their farmyard. When he brought the water he got an orange for it, a huge red Cretan orange, and looked amazed. His little sister stared. His face red, he sidled away, his orange safe behind his back. The little girl wailed. Their mother leaned out of a window shrilling, but he pretended not to hear. 'Milan! Milan! *Milan!*'

Milan smiled at us. A gold frieze of corncobs was hanging under their eaves. Snow in the mud, melting.

There could be a soul bursting up out of the bay that minute. There, that bubble of hurled light. How could you ever know? Like a shooting star, or lightning. People did drown in the bay, and lie sodden in the dark, hung in shrouds of seaweed. Fish grazed on them. One day they tumbled on to the beach at high tide and were found.

The soul itself might be only a metaphor. An image, a hope.

Do I have a soul, Mummy? She could imagine the child asking. Not yet, but in a few years. I don't know, sweet, she would answer. Nobody really knows. You *should* know, he would frown. Tell me. Yes or no? He hated uncertainty. He was like that. So had his father been.

'Mummy, I'm cold.'

On the way back the child went to the palm bole to visit his casemoth. It was gone. In the spurts of light from a failing streetlamp he found it at last on the tramline, crushed, its grey fuzz oozing thick orange-and-brown. He bent over it in disbelief, and his face crumpled and turned red. Tears splashed from his eyes.

'Look! Casemoss *died!*'

'Oh, yes, look. Oh, poor thing.'

'It's *died!* So you're a *liar!*'

She bought him an ice cream. It consoled him.

*

The brandy burned in her mouth and throat. She sniffed its hot breath over the rim. Glossy as honey, it cast its heavy light over her fingers.

Time was slower in solitude. There was the steady rise and fall of the sun, then the night. Time was *andante*.

The child lay warmly asleep at last.

Everything deteriorates, she thought. Nothing lasts. Flesh, and love, memories, relationships, the will to live.

Love also is an act of will. David doesn't love me. He has stopped loving his wife. Does she love him? I'm not allowed to know her name. Did I love Peter? It's nearly four years ago. Love too might be a metaphor.

We went to Mount Buffalo for our honeymoon. We walked to the Horn, the summit, in the sun, picking brown flowers. We nibbled raisins and oranges that spurted sour juice in our eyes. Crows croaked among the boulders. A dark thunderstorm struck. We ran to shelter in a hut sewn with cobwebs. Later we lay naked on a ledge of the Horn out of sight of the day trippers in cars. Far below us the trees were blue as mountains, and crows floated. Peter staggered laughing at the edge of the abyss until I screamed. In the flat grey of nightfall we walked down to the hut, drinking from a glassy trickle over dark rocks. We had a bright campfire and slept folded together on a bracken bed.

Later we camped on mountains in Greece, those grey-skinned mountains. We camped among silver olive trees and on river banks under the plane trees, in the sand and the brown leaves and the golden fur of their crushed seed balls. In crumbling fortresses sheep bells woke us. We slept on tideless pebble beaches and watched each morning as the sun erupted out of the yellow gulf. We drove to Italy, France, Germany, Austria. Yugoslavia.

The brandy stung her dry throat.

The road up from Titograd was narrow, pot-holed; a wreath at every bend marked a death. On a crest it was blocked by a heap of refrozen snow and as we skidded over it a timber lorry met us roaring round the white curve. Our car glided under the lorry, crumpling slowly. My head hit the dashboard. In amazement and rage, my head dripping, I heard our engine then the lorry's stop.

Peter was hanging over the steering wheel.

People had scurried from the buried farmhouses. Women helped me limp in. They made me coffee in a dark stuffy room, wrapped me in rugs and forced bristly grey gloves and socks on my hands and feet. They brought fried eggs and pickled cabbage, and thick glassy slivovitz. I drank that, but left the food. Curving my hands over my belly I showed them there was a baby. They made a compassionate whimpering as I lay curled on a sofa by the smoking stove. I woke with a sting, an ache, in my soggy head. It was bandaged. My hair was full of dry blood. A girl was there then who spoke English: Nada, her name was. Nada put her arm round me and told me that Peter had died. The sallow women cried drearily, plucking at their drab sweaty rags.

She sipped the burning brandy.

After her return she had written to Nada; after the formalities and the long flight; after the funeral. She had sent little presents. In return Nada had sent her cards that she had painted for the tourist trade. Snow, cottages by the road with golden windows and smoke coiling, icicles hung from their eaves. No wreaths where the road curved. No soul flung up in a shower of light out of all that snow.

Peter was reckless. He was happy–go–lucky. 'Hullo, you two happy–go–lucky young people,' a neighbour used to call as they went past. She never had been. She was the sensible one.

On the other side of the world, in the southern winter, the baby was safely born. She named him Peter Milan.

She took a last gulp of brandy and undressed. By lamplight white hairs at her temples glistened. Her eyes were bruised, but they always had been, all her life. Her teeth were patched and yellow–tinged. Rubbing oil on her legs these days, she could see the fine skin with its blue net of veins move, a milky plastic casing, over her shin bones. All over her the flesh was beginning to loosen like an old dress. Her elbows were sharp sockets, folded in shrivelled skin.

In his sleep the child chuckled.

'You fool,' she said to her yellow face, 'why did you put off going? How could you? Who will look after him if you die now?'

She laid her head beside his. His breath fluttered against her. She stroked his warm white arm downed

with silver hair. He rolled into her arms
   Someone will, she thought. My treasure, my darling.
My beautiful boy. Someone will look after you.

MARIA'S GIRL

I had not heard from my sister Maria for thirty years when a short letter in Greek arrived from Melbourne announcing her death of a brain tumour. Dear Uncle Manoli, it said. Her daughter, Niki, hoped her letter would find us. As the only child, she felt that she should let the family know. The name of the village had been on her mother's papers. She and a friend would be in Greece in January on their way to London and could come and visit us, if that was all right.

'Not a man friend, Manoli?' my wife said.

'It says *filo*. Yes.' I peered down at the letter. So Maria had had a child. 'Write to her, Vasso, will you. Tell her to come.'

Vasso sniffed. She wrote that same night.

After the letter the dreams began. I have seen others die Maria's death, slowly, in silence. Cancer eats the brain alive like wasp maggots in a spider. Her body, like mine, must have sagged, aged, all its hair gone grey. Grey corrugations mat my skull. My face is like a withering potato with white slit eyes. Night after night I shamble, my head thumping, to gape in a mirror aglare with yellow light at a grey face and blood-streaked eyes. Yet Maria in the dreams is twenty-six years old as I last saw her. Souls may not grow old when bodies do. I have a vision of yellow, speckled hands folded in death.

She was three years older, but once we were grown strangers often took us for twins. We lived here alone for a time, as close as twins. Our mother had died of pneumonia in the winter of '41. When our father was killed in the Civil War three years later I was still only sixteen. I carried my pistol everywhere. Relatives wanted to send us to the city, but we insisted we could manage. We treated each other, now I look back, with the tender respect of an engaged couple. Until the night of the fire.

Her guilt and shame forced her away. Not all at once, a gradual estrangement. As in a clear pane that crumbles before your eyes, the image beyond is lost in a mesh of white crystals.

When she left for Australia on the bride ship I went down to see her off, a gruff and grubby peasant jostled on the floodlit wharf with the city aunts and cousins. She was scarved and dressed in black, a widow already at twenty-six. Her eyes were wet. When my turn came to kiss her goodbye, she flinched. Neither of us ever wrote. Silence, for ever.

I watched the ship dwindle, flickering its golden lights.

Vasso must have noticed my dreams and wild awakenings, but we never discuss them, or much else these days but the goats and the firewood, the apple trees that need pruning, simple things. The violent years are behind us. Vasso has been a good wife and mother. She was always a cold woman, not like Maria, poor Vasso. If she has dreams of her own, she keeps them to herself. She is lonely now, I think. Each summer our sons arrive back in shiny cars from Munich and Zurich with their painted wives and little children. Each has named his eldest son and daughter after us. The children feed the hens and goats, chase fireflies on the river banks at nightfall, pick the fat, hairy mulberries, ride with me on the haycart. They cry when the time comes to leave. The little tragedies of children.

*

It is deep winter now. The river trickles, congealing, its banks heaped high with snow. The black trees could be wrought of ice and iron. Even at noon the whitewashed houses have lighted windows glowing under their crusted eaves, patching the snow with gold. The air is grey. In the yard our few white laying hens, almost invisible, jab at the frozen snow.

Niki is delighted with the snow.

Niki is just as I had imagined her, the image of Maria, the same age, and even dressed in black. The same golden skin and long, honey-coloured eyes and hair, banded hair glowing. How well I remember her, dressed for church, stooping low to iron the ends of her hair straight, the old flat-irons heating on the stove. She speaks good Greek in Maria's own voice. She is still wearing mourning for our sake, I think. It is our custom.

The whole village has exclaimed over the likeness, and made much of her. Only Vasso is critical at times, but Vasso is not from here. She never knew Maria. They are going on to London soon, anyway, Niki and her young man. They make no secret of sleeping in one bed, and stay there half the bitter white morning. Her Bill is forgiven a lot, not being Greek. He is well-liked, in fact, tall and blond, with his stutter and his glasses, his few words of Greek, his way of wheedling the old folk to pose for his camera with their carts and looms. In the *kafeneion* he buys beers all round and tries to dance to the juke box. They have been invited everywhere, even to the school. They are both schoolteachers. They are hoping to find jobs in London and come back to us in summer.

Over coffee the other day I showed them my old photograph of Maria and me on old Marko the horse in the vegetable patch. There was our old apricot tree, and the sunflower beside it, as tall as a man.

'Mama looked old, Theio. Older than you.'

'Well, she was three years older. But she was only twenty then. Our father had just died.'

'No, I mean now.'

Yet I know I look old for my age, though I am strong as rock.

'Fifty-six. That's not very old.'

'No. Poor Mama.' After a while, handing it back, she said, 'Is that a sunflower? Mama always had sunflowers in the garden.'

'It comes up every summer.' I wiped the .pane and pointed out the spot where it will rear its shaggy golden head. The snow fumed in a dark wind. Icicles glinted on the barbed wire fence. On all my land I see, with an inner eye, golden seeds lying in wait.

Niki is shocked by our poverty, the relentless cold dour poverty of our village. In the house we heat only one room, the front one with the old black fire-stove that lives on apple wood. Vasso grills bread and chestnuts on the top, boils the lentils and beans and an occasional hen, heats the bathwater, bakes her famous *pita* in its black depths. Vasso and I sleep in that room, and she takes the young ones a *mangali* of hot embers at bedtime, and squabbles when they open the window a crack behind the shutters.

'You'll catch your deaths!'

They look warm enough to me under Vasso's wedding *flokati*, like two humped, shaggy sheep, as she says good-night and switches the light off. What a blessing that we have electricity now.

Niki hates the way the hens dart in if the door opens and flap up on to the kitchen table to peck at bread and leftovers. When she chases them they squawk and rush around, skidding on their splayed claws and dropping brown splodges. The lavatory is a problem too, a concrete hole at the back, sheltered by plastic superphosphate bags hooked on blackberry brambles. There are always splodges of brown around its sloping mouth. In summer she will hate it even more, when the blackberries bring the wasps and glittering flies buzz in the hole. During the snowstorm the other day I said to go and do it in the barn. We all do. The goats don't mind, and the soiled straw will go on the fields anyway. No, she would squat outside in the storm with a sheet of plastic over her.

The animals make up for a lot, I think. She loves them all. Our wild yellow cat pads behind her, yowling. She feeds the goats and strokes their hot white pelts and long ears while they stand smiling and spry, fixing her with their slit gold eyes. I'm fond of the goats myself. Maria

loved them. How she mourned when they were taken in
the Civil War.

I showed Niki the soot still on the barn walls and asked
her if her mother had ever told her about the fire.

'No. You tell me, Theio.'

'Well, it was a long time ago.' I patted the hairy mud-
bricks. 'This was our house then, with rooms on top.
The Partisans burnt it in the Civil War. But no one was
hurt.'

The goats bowed and nudged me, the swollen pink
bags swinging between their legs. Niki's long-lidded
eyes betrayed disgust as I squatted to pump the teats with
these knotty old hands of mine. My hands are like tree-
roots, at home only in the soil. She's no good at milking.
You have to squeeze hard. Vasso has taught her to make
cheese.

Baths are a problem in winter, too, even once a week.
At first she wanted one every day, with the pipes frozen
and gallons being heated on the stove. One afternoon
soon after they arrived I tramped in from the barn, kicked
off my boots, and, hearing a voice call in the warm room,
naturally I flung the door open. The thought never
occurred to me. It wasn't a Saturday. I'm getting hard of
hearing now, besides.

She was stooping naked in the shallow copper pan that
we all use for baths, her hair in a coil at her nape, running
a shower of water from a saucepan over her long back.
Her black clothes off, she glowed all over with the gold of
ripened wheat.

'Maria!' I groaned.

But of course it was Niki who was crouching, turning
away, shame and outrage in her eyes. My blood froze. I
muttered an apology and slammed the door shut.

That night I dreamed of Maria as she stood naked in the
smouldering barn. Out of her bright hair burst the great
knuckly clusters of a brain tumour. She was weeping
black tears silently.

*

New horrors were just beginning then, as the Germans withdrew. Our father and other village authorities – our father had been mayor when we were little – were taken at gunpoint, tied up, marched up the mountain and threatened with death if they refused to join the Resistance. Some, who fell in their tracks, were shot where they lay. My father was shot escaping. Others who came back safe told me. My father, who had fought beside that Partisan leader on the Albanian front, would not fight against Greeks. Next, our animals were taken. Burnings had begun at night in villages in the foothills.

That day, I remember, Partisans from the mountain had made speeches in broad daylight in the square and withdrawn as night fell, but no further than the vineyard slopes across the river. The village hummed with fear behind closed doors. Thank God, a shepherd crept home after dark and gave the warning. Five houses were to be burnt. Ours was one.

I rushed Maria, empty-handed, stumbling and splashing, to our Uncle Stathi's house. He was alone, having sent our aunt and cousins weeks before to Thessaloniki. A lame, grey man stroking a rifle. We barred the doors and shutters and huddled there like roosting hens by lamplight. Hours went by before we saw through the slats a red flame on the sky.

Our uncle growled and cursed, swallowing great swigs of his *tsipouro* and thrusting the bottle at me. That was what I needed to make a man of me, he said. Harsh and fiery, the *tsipouro* made my blood beat hard. Maria, swaying, exclaimed and wailed. I sat with my arm round her, and could not have uttered a word if my life had been at stake. I have never spilt human blood.

When he sank back in a stupor we covered him up warm and crept with the lamp to our cousins' room. We rolled ourselves in blankets on the divans there, but we could not have slept. Maria was still making a sad whimpering.

'Maria? It's all right.'

'What can we do now, Manoli?'

'It's only a house. I'll build another one.'

'I'm too afraid.'

I could only just see her face by the dimmed lamp.

'Manoli?' she whispered. 'Can I get in with you?'

I nodded. She lifted the blanket and slid in against me, her hands on my shoulders. Transfixed with shock, I burned and ached, clenched against her. She kissed me with her tongue tasting of tears, and put my hands on her soft breasts and the long, furry lips between her thighs. When I went into her she grasped me with folded legs. Never since have I felt such joy and pain and terror with any woman.

Afterwards we lay still. Her long eyes were closed. Her hair had come undone and scarved my throat with hot, itching, amber swathes.

'Let me go. Oh, my God! It's a great sin. Manoli, no.'

'You don't love me?'

'Ssh. Yes. But you mustn't ever tell. Swear.'

'I swear. Are you sorry?'

She kissed me and moved away, smoothing my blanket down.

'Are you? Maria?'

'I don't know.'

It was my first time. I wanted to tell her, but her back was turned.

At some time the lamp sizzled and went out, I remember half-waking. We woke together much later, and, without disturbing Theio Stathi's snores we crept into the first blue light of day, trailing our white breaths, jumping as cocks crew. Our house was charred, smouldering. Beams protruded, black-blistered and gnawed. Shutters and window-panes lay smashed in the mud. I thought of unseen eyes following our backs through the hot doorway. A stench of kerosene. Our feet crunched on a black flood of wheat.

The old trunk with her wedding things in it had fallen through the burnt floor of the bedroom and lay burst open on a heap of ashes. With a cry she knelt and dragged out her ruined linens and sheets and hand-dyed woven blankets, the patient embroideries and laces of all her winters. She held up a singed cloth to show me. Black tears began to trickle down her face.

I hugged her then, both of us crouching as the darkness around us crackled and fumed. Wisps of flame still glowed here and there on black tufts of sacking. I found one of the crocks of water we always kept under there, wetted the cloth and wiped her face with it.

'Let me see you,' I muttered.

She shook her head, but did not resist as I took off her black clothes one by one until she stood there golden all over and I could touch her nipples and the curls of brown hair in her armpits and her groin that I had never seen before. Sudden voices and footsteps outside brought us to our senses. Frantically she pulled her clothes back on.

'Help me! Quick! Are my eyes red?'

She gave a sobbing laugh, and went out. Theio Stathi, haggard and vague, and all the family and neighbours had gathered in the yard, volubly indignant about the burning. They escorted us back with a chorus of commiserations. The sun came up and went down before they had all had their say. In the end it was decided that Maria must be sent out of harm's way to his sister-in-law the *modistra* in Athens, where she could learn dressmaking and earn her living keeping house. I sat there, struck dumb with anguish and bitterness, and not once did she look my way.

We were never alone again. They arranged a marriage for her down there, a ship's cook of forty who loved her madly, they said. I never met the man. It was at short notice, at the height of the Civil War. I rented her share of the fields from her and sent her the money. I visited her once, on business. There were others there. Numbly I watched this polite stranger fumbling with coffee cups. They had no children. When her husband's ship was lost at sea in '49 I bought her share so she could take a dowry to Australia. And for years I thought about her every night.

The new house I built has walls of stone one metre

thick. My shoulders will bear the scars of those stones to the grave. It is the bitterest thought to me that our sons will rush home and sell the house and land when we die.

*

Yesterday, as night drew in, we were sitting round the open stove in a firelight yellow as maize oil, eating the last wrinkled winter apples that Niki had roasted with honey. Bill sprawled, scribbling aerograms. Vasso was kneading a last *pita* for them. They are going in a day or two.

'It's been lovely, Theio. I'm glad I wrote.'

'Lucky you found the address. Where was it?'

'Oh, on her birth certificate,' she yawned. 'And she told me about her brother Manoli when she called my baby brother after you. She said you'd never leave here.'

I could only gape at that golden face.

'You didn't know? He only lived a few weeks. Something wrong with his heart. Mama was shattered. She called the *papas* to come and baptize him with the neighbours as godparents. Emmanuel, that's right, isn't it? After you.' She grimaced. 'My father was furious. His father's name was Yannis. He kept saying, "What right had you? What bloody right?"'

I poked sparks in the glowing apple wood.

'Were they happy together?'

'Sometimes.' She shrugged.

Last night, when I saw Maria, shreds of dead flesh hung from her, black shreds, and her black clothes. Her mouth gaped in silent shrieks. 'Manoli! Manoli!' Nothing I can say can comfort her. Throwing off the covers I stumbled shuddering outside into a black silence. The sky was hung with icicles and a white sickle moon. On the snow the shadows of trees lay in nets. A far wolf howled. Safe and warm, a goat whimpered in her sleep. My shaft of urine, glittering, pitted the white crust. Soon the thaw will set in. Heavy work brings heavy sleep. She has promised to come back to us in summer, Maria's girl has.

She will see the sunflower.

SLATE & ME
AND BLANCHE MCBRIDE

Georgia Savage

With the help of his younger brother, Wyn, Slate Jackson, home from Vietnam, robs a bank at Mowbray ·on the Murray.

During the robbery Wyn kills a policeman and is seen by schoolgirl, Blanche McBride. She is abducted by the men and taken across the river to a hideout.

From then on the balance of power between the three subtly shifts. One brother believes the girl is his because he's earned her. The other, ostensibly the tough one, becomes utterly obsessed with her and she with him.

Georgia Savage gets inside the heads of her characters to an astonishing degree and makes the sexual and romantic drama being played out between the three as gripping as the manhunt which finally breaks them all.